SWIFT DAM

SID GUSTAFSON

Published by Open Books

Cover image "Swift Dam on Birch Creek, Montana"
Copyright © Sam Beebe
Learn more about the artist at flickr.com/photos/sbeebe/

"To sleep, perchance to dream."
—William Shakespeare, *Hamlet*

For Rib

RAIN

Rain lulled them to sleep. The rain ceased and the sky cleared and in that hollow they slept. Silence held sway, save an occasional wisp of wind.

Later in the night, much later, the phone rang. And rang. The wife did not respond to nighttime ringings anymore. A certain part of Nan's sleeping subconscious had learnt to block the belling—seldom any good coming from that phone at night. On she slept, peace as if she not only lived in harmony with her husband, but in harmony with the world.

Sheriff Oberly opened his eyes. It was his Pondera County cell-phone, the link to Dispatch. Not a lot of folks had the number. Nan's hair lay across his face. He blew the tresses away and inhaled. He wedged his hand between the sheets and fingered the iPhone off the bed stand, sliding his thumb across the screen.

"Bird Oberly," he answered, licking his teeth, muffling the device over his lips. He listened. This wasn't Dispatch. The sheriff found himself fielding a missing-person report from a citizen. He slid his legs off the edge of the bed and placed the balls of his feet on the cold pine floor, flexing his toes. The seasoned sheriff concluded straightaway that his friend Doctor 'Fingers' Vallerone had driven into the mountains to spend the night, as had been his habit of late. He pinched the bridge of his nose to hear out the caller, Dr. Vallerone's son, Ricky.

The sheriff stood. He pictures the veterinarian parking his car at the base of Swift Dam. He imagines him sprawled out in the back seat of the sedan, fallen asleep under the monolith. On one of his recent sheriff runs to Swift Dam, he'd found him such. Oberly suspects Fingers might have dreamt through the rain, sleeping into the moonglow and now the moonshadow of Swift Dam. Nighthawking had become routine for Fingers of late. The veterinarian's nocturnal journeys didn't seem something law enforcement need be concerned.

For some reason, Ricky was determined to make a missing-person issue of this particular trip to Swift Dam, or wherever the veterinarian might have ventured. If not sleeping under Swift Dam, the doctor may well be out healing an animal in need. Sheriff Oberly might have expressed concern had he not known Ricky's father so well. It wasn't like Doctor Vallerone was some senile driving off and getting lost like he didn't know who he was or where he was headed. No, Doctor Fingers Vallerone was the most lucid of moondrivers, a pastime his veterinary profession nurtured through the years.

Nonetheless, Vallerone's youngest son insisted something was amiss, demanding official action be taken. Oberly ground his teeth. He did not appreciate being told how to proceed in matters of Pondera County law enforcement, not after three terms in office, and not about his friend Fingers Vallerone, even if the urging was from Vallerone's grown son.

The sheriff watched his wife's rhythmic breathing, jealous of her detachment. Oberly loved Nan. He tried to bring his breathing into cadence with hers, a calming technique the horse-medicine-man Many White Horses taught him long ago—a respired togetherness. Perhaps Bird Oberly had been sheriff long enough. Despite all his law enforcement training to handle stress with finesse, here he sat losing his calm over a phone call. Ricky must have lifted the number from his father, his dad being one of the few citizens of Pondera County that Bird shared his cell.

The call had taken Oberly out of a spacious dream, the water dream. The sheriff stretched. In the pauses of their many nights spent under the Rocky Mountain Front, Oberly and Vallerone came to share a multitude of notions. The two met travelling the backcountry ranches, stopping to visit whenever their paths crossed. They'd spent time together on the cattle-shipping circuit last fall, Doc writing the health certificates while Oberly performed the brand inspections—Montana calves shipping out to fatten on Illinois corn.

The sheriff glanced at his window to get a feel for the time of night. The sonata of late-evening rain had hypnotized Oberly into a loving yen with Nan, whirling his internal clock askew. Over the years, Oberly had become wary of phone calls. He once dreamt of receiving a phone call, getting up and going so far as to solve the crime, only to awaken in Nan's arms to discover it had all been a dream.

"You hearing me, Sheriff?" Ricky clucked.

This phone call was no dream. Bird extended his arm to visualize the iPhone screen. 4:12 am. He gazed back to his wife. He longed to re-spoon, to fasten and finish the water dream. If not children, the two had cultivated dreams through their years of marriage. Sleep had come to be the couple's favored refuge and sport—sleep. Unlike Vallerone, who appeared to favor sleeping solo, Oberly depended on his wife to mitigate the wrongs of the world.

"I'll check around, Ricky. See if I can locate your father. I'll get back to you when I find him."

Bird ended the call and blocked Ricky's number.

WATER

*F*ingers Vallerone parks under Swift Dam near the memorial erected by his two closest Indian friends, Howler Ground Owl and Many White Horses. It took three years for the two Blackfeet men to chisel and paint the pictograph on a boulder let loose from the Flood of '64, the same period of time it took the Pondera irrigators to replace the clay-footed barrier that gave way.

Vallerone steps out of his car and looks upward. He stares into the concrete face of Swift Dam. The geometric curve dizzies him. He fingers the words chiseled into the granite memorial as if reading Braille:

> *From water and mud Indians sprang.*
> *To water and mud many have returned.*
> *When the flow stops, the natives go with it.*
> *But the water flows on, and on.*

An artificial stream of water squirts out of the base of the dam, discharging the reservoir holding into a blue pool. The contrived water swirls to a ledge, spilling away to course the foothills a sterile streambed, water harnessed to irrigate monocultures beyond the reservation.

On the memorial boulder, a sheet of brass is fastened, tarnished with time. The engraved names fill with silt. Vallerone pulls a rag from his pocket and polishes the brass, taking care to shine Ivan Buffalo Heart's name. With a jugular needle, he scrapes the silt out of the letters. Rain falls, a hard rain falling as if it may never stop, Vallerone witness to the cold rain.

Above Swift, the Birch Creek drainages bear the precipitate waters that feed the reservoir. Diverse province of sheep and goat. Pristine realm of deer and grizzly. Sky of ravens and eagles—a wilderness spared the industry of man, a landscape once ruled by buffalo and wolves, tended by American Indians—the time before dams. Fingers' mind explores the drainages. Trips in and out with horses, children, and the Catholic. The time approaches where he may not be able to explore the backwaters anymore, evermore. He runs through each flow, his aging mind sharp, his memory a horse.

The soft-flowing South Fork waltzes through a grassy cottonwood valley before its run is buried in the reservoir. His string of horses conveys his brood of children through the drainage and into the wilderness.

Limestone waters stream down the Middle Fork, splashing off majestic cirques to join the South Fork. Fingers recalls trip after trip with horses into that amphitheater of stone, a precipitous nowhere land; province of wolverine, realm of lynx. The Middle Fork represents an empire of time—dwelling place of the Blackfeet spirits of yore.

The North Fork of Birch Creek enters the western arm of the reservoir, a freestone stream cutting a linear path from Badger Pass. His family of man and horses and dogs traverse this eastbound route home, making the loop from the west side through Big River Meadows and up Strawberry Creek. Rocky Mountain water carves through overthrust after overthrust displaying the salty history of the world. Trilobites. Horses then and memory now carry Vallerone through beginnings of time.

Early in Fingers' healing career, Many White Horses showed him the history of the land written in rock. Together, they spent days riding their horses searching for elusive pearls of stone. Up the North Fork, they discovered the fossilized opalescent sea-worms and the pleated clamshells of *Corbicula*. They searched for *Baculites compressus* of iniskim fame, the buffalo-calling stones used by the medicine men to lure the buffalo. Eons of Birch Creek flow have exposed the fossils the Indians still seek for guidance. Tributary streams transport windswept mountain silt, carrying the ancient seabed from mountains to plains, minerals to grow the grasses that once nourished buffalo, range now grazed by cattle and horses.

Wolves wander and pack together as they have through time, howling for lost brethren.

Fingers Vallerone howls in answer, he howls aloud the memory of the world the mountains hold, he howls for water that cannot flow. Wolves reply.

Vallerone howls in answer, he howls to know as wolves know, to learn, to see forever as wolves see, to hear. He transforms himself under the monolith, this concrete they call Swift, this pyramid they claim will be permanent this time, a construct that will not break and fold.

Vallerone knows better. He knows Father Time remains undefeated, his horses taught him, the wolves tell him so. Time wears by, time lit by a sliding moon, and Vallerone howls.

In 1914, Swift Dam went up a stone and boulder at a time, altering the Birch Creek tide of life. The manifest irrigators arrived with destiny on their shoulders; Europeans, Belgians and New Hollanders—Scandinavians with a knack and need to work land, the pastoral addiction to toil and sow; to take from the land, to stay and grow. They arrived with an itch for extraction, an obsession to make land arable. *Arabilis*, 'to plow.'

Water tripled and quadrupled the bounty extracted from a piece of land. Not without a price, no not without a price. The Earth and Indians pay the price. Father Time knows the price, Father Time and this man Alphonse Vallerone, the man the Indians call Fingers.

Instead of minerals ferried by natural flow to nourish the plains, the Birch Creek silt sifts to the bottom of Swift Reservoir. The flow of water stalls behind the earth fill. Life-giving particulates settle to the bottom. The floor of the reservoir is smothered in sandy hills, an artificial wasteland, a dead zone. No longer does the life-sustaining silt transcend the sacred cleft. No longer do these mountains mineralize the plains. The workings of time drift to the bottom of the reservoir to create the Sand Hills of Indian lore, Sand Hills exposed by the Flood of '64.

Before the dam gave way, Howler Ground Owl and his family ranched the riverbottom where the Blackfeet people had resided for centuries, ranching in their blood. Ivan Buffalo Heart, Tess' husband, tried to save Howler's family when the dam gave way, but no one was to be saved, every riverdweller drowned. The wall of water vanquished life altogether under the dam, Howler's children and wife washed away, Ivan with them.

Howler and his sister Tess were spared. Tess had driven the family Jeep out of the riverbottom before Swift gave way. She travelled the high road toward Dupuyer as Swift dissembled, drowning her husband and nieces and nephews. She'd left to see the Hutterites to barter for fresh vegetables to feed her clan. Her people raised cattle the Moravian Anabaptists prized for their vigor, and they in turn cultivated the fresh vegetables and grains her family needed. These socialists cultivated the land while Tess' nomads grazed cattle upcountry. The two cultures traded goods.

Tess drove for food. Howler travelled horseback above the floodplain, trotting up Sun Coulee to tend the cattle. Swift gave way.

THE BLACK BAG

*F*ull moons. Full moons and phone calls. Phones ring and moon-drivers drive, car-sleepers seek to understand times past, and life in Pondera County clocks forward. The consolation tonight was that of all the troubles Sheriff Bird Oberly might be called upon to resolve, Fingers Vallerone driving off into a fullmoon night was probably the least trouble of all. Vallerone's youngest son hadn't made this particular foray of his father's an easy trip to ignore.

Truth be known, the sheriff was pleased Ricky's father was out there keeping an eye on the night. Through times past, the sheriff and veterinarian shared a certain watch over Pondera County darkness. Some wear dimness fashionably, especially moonlit dim. Vallerone reflected moonshine with elegance. In Oberly's opinion, Fingers Vallerone played the most important night-wanderer since the Blackfeet Medicine Men of yore. Not only did Vallerone moondrive, he healed the animals and folk of the land, much as wandering healers have healed through time.

As long as domesticates have lived amidst mankind, gifted healers have restored the vigor depleted by human manipulation. Fingers mended and nourished animals up and down the Rocky Mountain Front, domestic animals living in a wild land not fully tamed. As he healed, he taught the animal keepers to see the world from their animals' viewpoint, both the domestic and wild perspective. Alphonse Vallerone, a medicine man of the oldest order, an intuitive physician.

The horse doctor began sleeping under the rebuilt Swift Dam when he found himself too exhausted to drive back to Conrad after his veterinary rounds to the West. Memories sleep with him under Swift Dam. Ever since he searched for the survivors of the Flood of '64, he harbors a privation to revisit the boulder-strewn aftermath.

Mornings under Swift Dam became Vallerone's affinity. He cherished dawn as the only part of the day that hadn't been purged by Manifest Destiny, a time that held the glimmer of eras past, the quiet. Through the decades, darkness had become the veterinarian's silent companion. His travel by night was rewarded with the reliable promise of morning. Witness to the lifting of darkness is a pleasure Doctor Vallerone will not be denied in his old age. He'd departed in the rain seeking moonlit darkness, and would return by sunlight.

The sheriff snaked out of the bedroom so as not to awaken his wife. He listened, absorbing the anger in the son's voice, anger about wealth, a short-changed son. Money caused much of Pondera County's troubles, and money seemed the thorn here. Back in the day, the veterinarian informed his family and staff of his destination each time he departed. Then, it was important that his office be able to contact him should another animal in need materialize near his ministrations. In those days, rather than money being money, time was money. If the veterinarian could save a second trip 60 miles north by letting folks know where he was headed, all the better. Vallerone aspired to veterinary efficiency. For decades, he made himself available 24/7 to keep his agribusiness

12

flowing. He worked hard to please his wife and raise his boys and get them through college, and had.

These days, Vallerone wanted left alone. When cell phones became popular, and then essential, Fingers Vallerone refused to acquire one. He had been through the ringer of techno-availability, if not the Golden Triangle pioneer of it. In the 60s he had a two-way radio built into his veterinary car. This device transformed his yellow Impala to animal ambulance. Vallerone became Dr. Available. His life became one travelling emergency after another at the behest of radio wave transmissions.

The cow doctor came to be called Grasshopper by the Babb Indians in Happy Valley, his radio antennae noticeable to these folk. The way he hopped around the countryside, the handle fit. In the 70s, as if the two-way radio of the 60s did not offer availability enough, he became the first veterinarian to have a mobile phone installed in his car, the first of its kind; push button dial, speaker, the works. Dr. Vallerone single-handedly managed the animal health of the Reservation borderland with Canada, and his phone facilitated the timely transport of healthy beef.

Sheriff Oberly appreciated the relief the aging veterinarian must feel to at last be unavailable, to be irretrievable—the dream of many a country veterinarian through time—the dream of many a Pondera County sheriff. Bird knew Vallerone had planned this fullmoon night to dream uninterrupted; to embrace a personal freedom denied in his home in Conrad. He took flight to locate the perspective he needed to carry on, a practice learnt from Indians.

The son—while not outright declaring it—seemed more concerned about the black bag than his father's well-being. Oberly surmised that Fingers had again departed with the leather bag—a supposed bag of money—the Pondera folktale that had not found credence with the sheriff, a full bag carted out of the bank to the Blackfeet

Indian Reservation. Conventional wisdom holds that horse doctors have carried all sorts of bags through time—that identifying tote of their healing profession, the collection of scopes, instruments, and galenicals that diagnose, relieve, and cure—the healing bag. Those were the days, practicing medicine out of a bag.

The sheriff knew of another black bag, the bag that stored the harpoons and wide-gauge needles to administer the Sleepaway pentobarbital solution—the "sleeping bag," as Doc dubbed it, a bag black as bags come. Generally, when that medical bag surfaced, hush followed. That was the black bag Oberly knew. As close as the two night-lifers were, the sheriff had never seen any black bag other than the Sleepaway bag. It made perfect black-bag sense that Dr. Vallerone might not declare his intended destination if indeed he had to bring that wretched bag along. If he had departed on a mission to facilitate a crossover, the sheriff respected unavailability. Trips with the black bag in hand needed no probing from Bird Oberly. If Fingers happened off in the night with such a bag in hand, who could expect him to explain why and where? Not Indian O. The sheriff had no evidence regarding bagged money, dark or otherwise. Money had not been reported missing or mishandled, not by Dr. Vallerone.

Maybe Doc kept the *Nembutal* in the bank vault. Controlled drugs were, after all, to be kept under lock and key. His supply was once stolen from the vet clinic. And if the bag transported money, money for what? Sheriffs require motives. Oberly could find no motive for Vallerone to mule money, drugs, or anything else. What could money buy up Swift way, cash money at that? Horses could be bought for cash, cows not so easy. Hay, maybe the cash was for hay, as cash bought hay more easily than checks or promises bought hay. Vallerone was putting a little herd of cows together, after all. And then he had the thoroughbred band of hopeful racehorses to feed all winter. One needed to stockpile hay to run cows and horses in these parts, and hay cost money.

One jellyfish suggested the veterinarian was running livestock medications. The rancher—upset that Doc wouldn't supply him with prescription drugs as ordered— insinuated Doc had a therapeutic drug cartel going, smuggling the goods down from Canada, a country where new drugs sometimes came sooner available than the more proven American drugs. Where animal drugs were needed in volume, animal welfare suffered. Oberly knew Vallerone would never support that. He taught folks how to ranch without drugs, rather than with them. He left pharmaceutical scrimming to the new veterinarians canvassing the landscape, veterinarians who slept with their phones turned off.

Without a motive for the transport of money, the black bag was out of Oberly's lean. The locals could speculate all they wanted about black bags. Until Oberly had evidence or a motive, he'd leave Vallerone's alleged black bag uncharted ground. Vallerone was said to have money these days, more money than ever, but money hadn't changed him like money changed others. Fingers had never been about money. As far as Oberly was concerned, he never would be; modest house, modest life; modest car, modest wife. Lived the same non-material life that he had before coming into his supposed publishing wealth.

Modest father. Immodest son. Black bag.

Oberly conceded that maybe the veterinarian was off with a black bag of some sort, but so what? Nothing new. Black bag or not, O knew that Fingers was off doing something he needed to do, be it dream or heal or facilitate deliverance.

Oberly's house phone rang. He was too contactable. Ricky had all the phone numbers. Most everyone in Pondera County probably had them.

The son started in with maladies: "He's been sleeping a lot. He's sick with something. You have to go find him."

"The old are said to need lots of sleep, Rick."

"He sleeps all day."

"Perhaps because he is up all night..."

"He's losing his edge. Dad has gone a bit off a bit; lately he has."

"Are you sure you're okay, Ricky?" Oberly rejoined, putting a big U in the 'you're,' suggesting the son's mental health might be amuck rather than the father's, a diversion measure he'd been taught at sheriff school to stifle morbid speculation. Oberly had become a well-educated, professionally-trained lawman, having attended many domestic-dispute workshops in his ascent up the muddy slope of law enforcement. He slid his arms into his bathrobe and walked into his living room, listening, always listening, a requirement of sheriff-hood.

The view relaxed him. His picture window revealed the splendor of the Rocky Mountain Front, the love bubble fallen low, its roundness plumped by some optical effect of atmosphere. In whatever silvered canyon Fingers had spent the night, he'd had a fine moon to rabbit his dreams.

The clouds must have cleared by midnight. With such luminosity it couldn't have been such a long night, and certainly didn't seem one now. The dreams dreamt must have been insightful. How could they have been otherwise? The shortest night of the year was a few weeks away, this morning's sunrise not far off. With morning comes revelation, and promise. Enlightenment.

The son begged: "Come on, sheriff. Get a search and rescue going. He's been gone too long!"

The sheriff remained silent.

"I know your Indian people go off for days at a time without a second thought, but this isn't the rez."

At the same conferences that taught Tazering and cuffing, Oberly learned to ignore ignorant comments. If white folk considered themselves above the Indian, Oberly could play the Sitting Bull game, and play it well. People in Pondera County had to take care what they said and how they thought around Sheriff Oberly. This Indian could tell what white people thought, not because they thought out loud—although they did enough of that—but because Oberly could see what white folk thought by how they walked. Oberly knew kinetic empathy, the method by which wolves and horses communicate, a gesture language he attained fluency in long ago.

In addition to understanding the language of movement like a horse, Bird Oberly had a memory like one. Few could put anything past Sheriff O. If one did, Bird could exact retribution like a mule—an advantage to maintain lawfulness. If someone let slip with an apple comment around the sheriff, they could not expect leeway on any future points of the law. No rolling through stop signs, no lead-footed travel, no drunken mistakes forgiven. Many did jail time for certain words uttered, certain thoughts walked.

The sheriff set Ricky's kin comment aside, puzzled as to how Vallerone's offspring could be prejudiced. Fingers Vallerone found asylum with the Indians, his preferred animal folk. Howler and Tess' merger with horses beguiled him. In addition to practicing veterinary medicine, Vallerone observed and recorded the social nature of horses, the domesticated sharing of social constructs— communal group survival with the grass people. His writing documented the merging of horses with humans. In the shadow of his veterinary degree, with the help of Many White Horses, Dr. V acquired a position instructing Equine Behavior at the tribal college in Browning. After learning the nature of horses from the Indians, he now taught them the evolutionary basis of that nature. The blending of horses and humans entranced the man. If Fingers wasn't camped under the dolmen, he was under the spell of Howler and the thoroughbreds.

Perhaps the chestnut mare had foaled. Vallerone treasured watching each mare foal from a distance. He'd been known to stay afield for days waiting out a mare, a tough proposition, waiting out a mare. He hoped to find a correlation between how a mare taught the foal to be a horse in the first few hours of life, and how the foal performed later as a runner at the track. Fingers acquired a special spotting scope to observe the parturition of his mares from afar. He had come to know where and when they foaled in the open country of Tess' range. Vallerone sought to raise a classic winner someday. He yearned to know what made a foal a runner.

It might have been too late in his life to cattle ranch, but to breed a Derby runner; it was never too late for that. Old men bred Derby horses, wise old men; horsemen. After he came into money, he journeyed to purchase gravid mares in Kentucky. Each year he found two or three Jockey Club mares in foal to the best stallions he could manage. Sometimes he picked them up in Canada or California. He purchased mares in pairs, sometimes a band of three or four. He picked up late foalers, broodmares well-suited to foal in Montana in May or June on green grass. He treasured raising the thoroughbreds with Howler's band of Indian broodmares. He had bred and raised two ungraded stakes winners, no small feat from the hinterlands of Montana. Bigger races had so far eluded him, but the Kentucky Derby twinkled in his eyes.

He persevered. For a song, he purchased mares deemed infertile by Kentucky broodmare specialists. For Vallerone, the mares produced. Green grass, a free-roaming herd, and his Caslick's surgery cured many an infertile bloodhorse. He scrutinized trends. During certain years, valued bloodlines fell out of fashion to be let go softly. He treasured foaling on Front Range foothill grass. He theorized the best place for a Derby horse to learn the confidence and agility to run by and through other racehorses is at speed with the family band. Medaglia d' Oro was born in Kentucky but raised in Montana to become a premier runner, and later a leading sire. Vallerone gave his foals the opportunity to hone a running style in the open country of their ancestors. By the time

18

they made it to the track, they were all about run. Someday, someday. Vallerone dreamed someday.

The troubled son persisted. "Send a search party."

"A search party?" The sheriff winced as he considered all the people he'd have to call to instigate a search party. "What would your dad think of a missing-person's expedition on his behalf? Not much, Ricky, not much, I'm telling you."

Ricky tried to say something, but Oberly talked over him. "He's likely just fine, the way I see it. We'll wait him out. Give him some time."

"Easy for you to wait, isn't it?"

"Be reasonable, Ricky. I've waited out many a man. Simpler than waiting out a woman."

"This isn't about women," Ricky sniped.

"Everything is about women," the sheriff corrected. "Only a few hours until first light. Your father's spent many a night under these stars. He's either doing vet work, watching horses, or sleeping in his car. He'll return in better shape than he departed, I assure you."

"He'd a told us had he planned on staying out all night."

"You go find him, then. He's camped under Swift. If you want him, drive out and get him. If he's not there, I'll go find him myself. How's that?"

"You sure know a lot about my father."

"I'm paid to know about the citizens of Pondera County."

"He's seventy-seven. Not wise to gamble with a man's life at that age."

"Penning them up at home is the bigger gamble, I'd say."

"If anything happens—"

"What can happen? People get sleepy as they age. They drive off to look their life over, reach back for time left behind. Your dad goes off like this often, and you know it."

"It's freezing out there."

Oberly looked out there. Mountains attentive as his wife's breasts, the moon swollen as she nestled behind the Front. Foothill grass flaxen as her hair. He walked to his weather station. "Forty-four degrees at my place," Oberly reported. "Twenty mile-an-hour southwesterly wind, gusts to thirty-five. A Chinook of sorts, I'd say."

"Seventy-seven years of age."

"Gettin' up there all right."

"He could die out there."

"All find their time and place," Oberly replied, knowing it to be a comment Fingers said over many a death. The veterinarian and the sheriff had shared death together many a night during their Conrad careers. Life and death beheld the pair more than life and death beheld average others. The sheriff and the veterinarian met time and again over death. They confronted death, and death them. Knowing death, they did not fear death as others feared death. They encountered more life than death, and in the end, life outlives death.

"You'll regret saying that if Dad ends up dead out there."

"Not likely he'll end up dead out there, Ricky, not likely at all. He takes pretty good care of himself. Especially at night. Always brings food, water, and blankets. His whole trunk is a first aid kit for man or beast. I know your father. He'll be fine."

"What is it that makes you so clairvoyant about my father, sheriff?"

"We sometimes attend church together."

"I heard you two worship Buddha."

"And Crazy Horse. Others. Napi mostly."

Last year, Vallerone recruited a monk he'd met in Glacier Park to host a retreat up at the Pine Butte Nature Preserve. Oberly brought down some traditional Blackfeet medicine men, Many White Horses and others. They celebrated 'religions of the earth people.' Animal and parental connectivity took up the discussions. Oberly never knew his own father. His Uncle Howler threw in raising him, but he felt he never had a real father like other kids had a real father. The phone call was getting heavy. The sheriff realized he would not only have to deal with Ricky if Fingers did not emerge from the night by morning, he would have to deal with all of Ricky's pencil-dick acquaintances.

"Out-all-night is where I draw the line these days," Ricky declared.

"Not out-all-night just yet," the sheriff specified. "A few more hours of night remain. Dawn is his favorite space and you know it. Let him enjoy the daybreak."

Oberly envied the lost doctor. He gazed to the Front. "A sweet moonlit night after such a cleansing evening rain. Ricky, do you see that moonset?"

"No, I don't see the moon. I don't care about the moonset," he replied.

People who didn't pay attention to the moon disappointed Oberly. "I'll start a search if he doesn't arrive by... let's say... noon."

The sheriff grinned and pictured Fingers rolling into town, his Crown Vic travelling low and dusted, his hair mussed, a smile ragged and real. If a vet call had drawn him into the night, there might be flecks of blood on his cheeks and clothes. If he'd been inside a cow to his elbows, blood sometimes remained on the back of his arms. Blood interested the sheriff. But Vallerone's blood had always been cow blood, or horse. Animal blood dried to a different color than human blood, and from his encounters with Vallerone, Oberly had learned to distinguish human blood from other blood. Crime labs backed up this penchant of his—a reader of blood, Bird Oberly.

If not sleeping under Swift Dam, Vallerone might be tending a swift horse. Practiced ranchers knew where to find the seasoned veterinarian. He may not have enamored every client with his intuitive acumen, but for those ranchers with whom Vallerone clicked—and there lived more than a few—the horse doctor had a lifetime of work ahead.

At seventy-seven, Fingers remained game as ever to eye a lameness. He carried with him the tools to stitch lacerations, the drugs to painlessly slice into the next heifer to deliver the next newborn into a cold, hard world. Doc had long delved into those placental caverns where survival traits are handed down from generation to generation, and he will delve more before this story is told. He taught his ranchers the principles of genetics. To Dr. Vallerone's credit, cesareans became a need of the past. Heifers were bred to birth easily these days, and only in rare cases of malpresentations, breeches, and the like, was Vallerone called in with the scalpel.

In his travels to animals in need, Doc perfected moondriving. He had to, to survive. Before his Crown Victoria years of late, his vehicle of choice into the 70s was the Chevrolet Impala, the manual transmission model with the shifter on the steering column, a three-speed. Traction, Fingers Vallerone claimed the cars had better traction than the weak-travelling pickups of the day. He freewheeled his laden rig over the countryside from horse to cow, all those foothill ridges and prairies, all those snowy roads. His mission: bringing life into the world. Not dust, gravel, mud, blood, or night can keep Fingers Vallerone from delivering life. Being witness to all those first breaths drew him on, so many more waiting to breathe. All the suck reflexes he induced, all the ligatures he tied and salves he ministered, all those infusions and injections that healed and cured. Vallerone gave all, no better giving than helping the people of this world with their animals, no better vocation for this foothill veterinarian. Vallerone would know no other, save his prose. He embraced his work delivering life, all a doctor can ask—the animals he tended fortunate, the ranchers more so. Saving lives fueled his human needs, most of them.

"Something might happen by dawn, sheriff. Something might have happened already," Rick said.

"Nothing's happened."

"Best you do something," he commanded. "You could end up losing the primary on account of this bullshit you're pulling!"

The election. Now, as added weight to his law enforcement duties, the sheriff had to deal with threats regarding the impending election. Oberly had had enough. "I'll take care of it my way," Bird stated. "Vote for whom pleases you. I've got your father covered." Click.

Let 'em vote me out, O smiled. Let some other fool field this moon work. Ranching is my destiny. Vote me out in the primary and don't expect to hear the lame duck quack. As it was and always had been, Oberly needed his sheriff's salary and benefits. Money, money to feed the needs of his younger wife, money saved for the family they both dreamed, clock-ticking, money to cobble together a ranch to raise the children amongst the animals on the land. Money, land, kids. The sheriff imagined finding a suitcase full of money in some borrow pit on his highway rounds, money looking for a home, money seeking family.

He walked back to the bedroom to watch his wife. He pondered other professions. It seems his sheriffing may be the cause of their barrenness, nights like this. He considered moving Nan to Birch Creek, a return to Indian living: training horses, herding cattle, mating heifers, making hay. Living alongside the animals on the land, answering to their needs rather than human desires, a dream of many a Montana man. Ranching would be conducive to fecundity, an erotic privacy deep and lost in grass.

Doc and Oberly considered cobbling together a ranching operation. After the completion of their varied nighttime dealings with troubled folk and their troubled stock, they'd take in the air and consider joining the cattle-raising fray. Oberly's salary could never fund a ranch, but Fingers veterinary practice had fiscal possibilities, especially of late. Oberly thought he might someday set up a headquarters at Howler and his mother's place. They had the riverbottom acres, not enough land to carry a herd of cattle and horses year round, but a home place to harvest a hay crop to winter the herd, if only they could secure summer grass.

Dr. Vallerone had capital and collateral. He held deed on his wife's residence in town, four lots with that view of the Rockies, plus a twelve-acre tract of commercial land surrounding his remodeled veterinary clinic near I-15. He and Maple possessed a string of rental houses, the houses where Vallerone housed orphans of the land through the years.

Oberly thought a ranch possible for Doc, but at seventy-seven, it was too late. No, on reconsideration, it wasn't too late. He was old, but not that old, not so old to not know how to enjoy hands-on ranching for another decade. Grandkids with a ranching interest could emerge. Vallerone had horses enough to ranch, and ranch big.

The wind softened. The sheriff walked into the den to wait the wandering Fingers Vallerone out.

SPIRIT

*F*rom the east, light.

Sun swarmed Oberly's face, heating him awake. The sheriff shielded his eyes with outreached palms, took his bearings, and summoned up the missing-person trouble. He stretched, happy to be waiting the veterinarian out, unhappy the call had interrupted his night. He would hold off reporting the incident to Dispatch until he checked in at the cafe where his most-trusted informants drank coffee. By 8 o'clock, Betty's dining patrons would be caffeinated and ready to inform him of all the pertinent sightings—the waitresses themselves most informative, informative because they hoped Bird might someday help them out of a jam as he had helped out so many locals. He was a handsome man. He sported a helpful native nature. His walk commanded calm, eyes beholding order. To consider Sheriff Oberly in his creased pants behind his shiny badge was to consider justice a fair and noble devotion.

The sheriff recalled Vallerone's younger days, a less-complicated time when the vet plucked him off the street, recruiting him to chauffeur him around the countryside.

Vallerone elevated Bird in the community as his able assistant, a friendship lasting decades. As Fingers' driver, Oberly came to appreciate the world through the eyes of animals at the hand of man, for better and for worse in the shadow of his Blackfeet animal culture.

It appeared to some to be a progressive time in Pondera County, the patrons of animal husbandry making a decent living on the land, fancy cows aplenty to command modern veterinary care, wheat enough to pay the bills. Oberly witnessed the price the animals paid for their keeper's prosperity. Conrad prospered, irrigated hay and wheat providing a rich bounty. To the west, the panhandle offered the finest grazing on the continent. With buffalo extirpated, the economic pursuit the un-irrigated land could best bear was the grazing of cattle. Cattle replaced the bison, the wolves shifted into the mountains, and the Indians tended cattle to native grass. Vallerone helped ranchers storm-proof their herds. He culled the weak, cured their empty and lame. He trained his clients to nourish their herds to withstand the winters, to wean early and let the cows fatten on the plentiful autumn grass, the rancher's prime resource. He recruited cattle buyers that paid a premium price for the quality calves he cultivated, and for a time dabbled as a cattle buyer himself. He designed cow-friendly handling facilities, and showed his clients the art of clean calving. He savored life as a cow doctor.

Pondera County flourished. After the Vietnam War, the taste for American beef became insatiable, a burger joint on every main street and interchange in America. Conrad herself had half a dozen; a Tastee-Freeze, an A&W, The Home Café, The Silver Moon, The Keg, and Betty's Diner, along with the Country Club. The Target and The Conrad Hotel served finer cuts. Vallerone's reservation calves became legendary beef, hardened calves that blossomed on Midwest corn, gaining, marbling readily, inhaled deliciously. Veterinary medicine evolved to support the industry; calves weaned, cows pregnancy tested, protected, and injected.

Oberly chucked firewood into the woodstove, lit the local news to fire the kindling, and flopped. Muffled in his bathrobe, he absorbed the crackling heat. He dozed in and out of driving Dr. Vallerone. Oberly knew the Blackfeet Reservation, and it was into that miasma of survivalists that Oberly guided the veterinarian. Animals connected Indians to the land, enchanting Fingers. Oberly's Indian awareness mixed with Fingers' animal insight facilitated healing. The advantage came in Oberly's ability to calm troubled horses in need of stitching, to ease the worried cow down an alleyway to be treated. Bird had the talent to convince an animal that needles were harmless if not helpful, which in Vallerone's hands most certainly were. Bird softened fear. He taught Fingers to take his time with cattle and horses.

Fingers relished Indian time, that native state where time is nothing, no clock but the sun. Lots of time in this world, lots of daylight, lots more time than the drowned will ever have. Animals taught Vallerone all about time. "Time is a horse's friend," Bird explained. "Horses need time. Cattle need time. We all need time. Let the horse smell everything, give her time. Let her smell your tools, your needles. Let her know your intent."

Fingers appreciated science, and Bird connected science to the horses. Bird possessed a genetic memory of horses. Blackfeet Indian ancestors arrived with their families and dogs before horses disappeared from this continent. It seemed possible Blackfeet ancestors knew the horse before the horse disappeared ten thousand years ago.

Like the white orphan of the smallpox story showing up to resurrect Indian culture, the white veterinarian arrived to resurrect an animal life on the land for the natives. Vallerone restored animal husbandry on the reservation, an art the Indians struggled to know in the face of lost buffalo. With Oberly at his side, Fingers had a true introduction to the veterinary life, a clean practice where Indians and animals prevailed. On the Blackfeet Nation and beyond, Fingers became the renowned Horse Medicine Man, a healer of horses and mender of cows, a coup he could not have attained without the animal guidance of Bird Oberly. If the two didn't follow God's livestock policy, they embraced Napi's.

The sheriff opens his eyes.

The wind picks up outside as wind picks up in changing light, dawn drawing wind across the world. The land wears out and its people and animals get old and die, but the wind blows forever.

He sees the blue sky and chants a prayer asking first light to awaken Fingers Alphonse Vallerone, an Indian song to guide the horse doctor back home to his waiting people...he hums the prayer again and again...a prayer his grandmother taught him up Heart Butte way... a prayer bringing many a warrior home... a song to be sung as night moves into first light.

Light floods the foothills like water flooded the Birch Valley that morning fifty years ago to the day in '64. At the thought of flood, O marches about his house worrying that Fingers' disappearance might create a mess of paperwork. Bird hates paper. It is always best for the Blackfeet Indian if there is no paperwork, best certain incidents remained undocumented.

The election gnawed on him, Oberly letting it gnaw knowing he shouldn't. He didn't appreciate the way certain voters hovered over his official duties. He hated scrutiny and despised accusations. Now, he was expected to keep the peace while contending with his first opponent in three terms, an opponent who filed against him in the primary election—a former deputy from his department vying for his position, a connected son of the soil.

When this development came down, insinuations surfaced regarding Oberly's reservation connections, and disconnections. A probe of his ability to solve crimes circulated. Oberly always seemed able to weather Conrad's local bias. Centuries back, when white people first arrived with their Bibles in hand, the Blackfeet reigned over the land and water and creatures of the region. These days the Blackfeet have the Bible and the white people have the land and water. As his time in office wore on, effective blunting of the prejudices he'd originally overcome to become sheriff seemed harder to stomach. His latest incumbency had its failures: a murder committed yet unsolved, a missing person unfound.

Mrs. Oberly moaned as her husband wedged his cold feet back between the sheets. Oberly often coupled with his wife after nighttime disturbances. She liked it and he liked it. She was often half-asleep, and it felt like he was taking her in a dream, which aroused him even more. The phone—a ringing in the night—became a conditioned stimulus for the wife; at least that was Oberly's hypothesis after years of sleeptime ringings. He imagined the longer he let the phone ring before he answered, the better the sexual resonance afterwards.

The wile had the added benefit of simmering down anxious callers. By the time Bird picked up, the complainant was grateful he'd answered at all, and the wife... the wife was subconsciously preparing herself. Sex cleared Oberly's tubes, allowing his forensic mind to relax, marital accord to help resolve the Pondera County problems that awaited his resolution. Nan was the daughter of a local rancher, an Irish lass he'd met in Dupuyer. As a teenager, Oberly came to live in the bunkhouse of her father's ranch, an Indian hand hired to put up irrigated hay, Nan years his junior.

It was with Dr. Vallerone that Oberly first discussed the Pavlovian arousal aspect of sleeptime phone rings and wives, the veterinarian no stranger to midnight calls himself. Their Pavlovian ruminations began years ago over a dead horse, the two rousted out of the sack by Dispatch a summer long ago. The two arrived to find the creature hit by a car and shot in the head, shot in the head by a trucker who'd stopped to help. Downed horse, wrecked car, no one hurt but the horse, the scent of rimfire in the air, the horse surviving the gunshot. The deputy stood on one side of the horse keeping the onlookers at bay while the vet went for his black bag. The trucker's bullet hadn't penetrated the brain. The horse seized, bleeding out her nostrils, galloping on her side. Doc loaded a jumbo syringe with barbiturate and harpooned the horse's jugular vein, Sleepaway taking the horse to the ultimate grass beyond. A deep last sigh and the horse strode from this world to the next.

Death cleared the crowd. The night-travellers shuffled to their cars and trucks. Doors slammed, engines fired, headlights brightened; onlookers fled as if the beast had succumbed to contagious distemper rather than Fingers' intravenous coup de grâce.

Deputy Oberly and Dr. Death stood in the night, abandoned. Appointed executioners, and now executors of the road-hit horse. Their respective professions delegated them resolvers of such misfortune. Had Fingers not been there, Oberly would have had to deliver the horse to the other side with his Glock .45. Oberly was as deft with his bullets as Doc was with his needle when it came to taking horses out, but with the crowd and the failure of the first bullet, Doc shouldered the duty.

The two men stood watching the cars pull away, including the car that had hit the horse, a bent Lincoln Continental, a dentist who wore his seatbelt. Everyone who drove far enough across netherland Montana eventually collided with livestock or wildlife. Care had to be taken not to overdrive one's headlights. Knowledge of the countryside habitat was helpful—knowing where the deer lived and drank, knowing their crossings, the grazing patterns of cattle and horses.

Dr. Vallerone dragged the winch and chain out of his car's trunk, a compartment storing all the tools of the veterinary trade. Vallerone tended to death as he tended to life, meticulously. A veterinarian's job was never over. Death halted nothing. Causes had to be determined, cures rendered for those still living. He fastened the chain to the dead horse, knowing the bones to hitch and knots to throw. Deputy Oberly secured the jack to a corner post and began cranking. Fingers guided the dead weight along with pulls and tugs on the taunt chain, coaxing the carcass down and across the barrow pit. He knew the geometric tricks and advantageous angles needed to move a dead horse.

After the two horsemen had removed the horse from the roadway, they stopped to rest and take in the empty night. Headlights gone, night windless and moonlit, eyes acclimated to the silvered darkness. The horse lay wide-eyed, pupils fixed and dilated, retinas reflecting the moon. The horse's pair-bonded other whinnied in the distance, calling her deceased friend.

"Poor sister," Oberly said, feeling for the surviving horse.

Fingers' gravelly voice soothed the mournful neighs: "Horse has the biggest mammalian eye on the planet. Sees as well as any predator, good as a cat at night... not an eye evolved to measure high-velocity headlights, though. Deer likewise. The predators are not so highway savvy, either."

The sheriff did not reply. He knew not to agree or disagree with the veterinarian as the man preached over his dead. He had learned to listen to Doc in the presence of animals. Vallerone the animal preacher held ideas and views that interested Oberly. Fingers held forth regular with those ideas over death, and birth, knowing Oberly listened as Indians listened to animal talk.

"In Kentucky, they bury the head, heart, and hooves of

a dead horse in a limestone hole."

"And the torso?"

"Rendered."

The borrow-pit horse's colon groaned from within.

"Long way from Kentucky," Oberly replied, standing hat in hand. "Magpies and coyotes will get this one, head, heart, hooves and all."

"We ought to bury her so the medicine I used to send her doesn't poison the wildlife," Vallerone replied.

"You should have told me that before you gaffed her. I could have shot her so she could feed the hungry."

"Thanks. The crowd wasn't ready for that. Next time death will be all yours."

The horse's pair-bonded friend continued whinnying from the field afar—stuttering, lonesome neighs. Another horse whinnied. In unison, the herd galloped off. Their crescendo of hooves circled to a halt, stopping across the fence to watch the men.

Fingers pondered the horse's final years, a life in the mountain foothills on the last of the native Great Plains. Horse heaven. Not only did the paleontologists marvel at the dinosaur bones excavated in these parts, they marveled at the wide array of fossilized horse bones discovered up and down the Front. The Rocky Mountain turf harbored the history of horses, and would soon harbor one more.

Oberly felt the horse's shoulder and hip for a brand. "Nothing. Slick as sin."

Fingers lifted the upper lip and shone his penlight on upper gum; a tattoo, K 45208, a Jockey Club runner, a thoroughbred, a horse who has seen it all, plains to stable, and back to the plains. Grass, horses are always after the best grass. Deprived of green grass during the racetrack years, she was drawn to the fresh road grass, the new grass, the best grazing. A last nipped mouthful rested in the corner of her lip.

"Grass. The gold is in the grass, the native grass," Vallerone said.

Vallerone bade the *Equus caballus* 'La Corredera' farewell, giving her the Spanish name for Runner. In his racetracks days, he spoke Spanish with the *caballerangos*. He adored the horse language the grooms spoke. As eulogy for La Corredera, he told the story of a Montana-bred who found lasting fame as a runner. Spokane holds the record for the mile and a half classic distance of the Kentucky Derby run in 1889. The race is now run at a mile and a quarter. "Shortening the distance has weakened the thoroughbred breed ever since," Vallerone pined. Of all things horse, Vallerone knew endurance. He understood wind. "Distance enhances wind. Pulmonary health reflects overall soundness. Healthy lungs oxygenate healthy legs. Horses are born to move. For a horse, to move is to breath, to breath is to run."

Vallerone admires horses with wind.

"Lungs make a racehorse. Miles and miles of daily walking are required to keep lungs resilient." Vallerone pushed the chest of La Corredera. "Beautiful lungs, look at her depth." He ran his hand over her thorax, withers to sternum. "To condition the lungs is to condition the joints." He flexed her knee, feeling the carpal bones. "Walking sustains soundness of both wind and limb. They don't walk racehorses like they used to, like they should. Instead of conditioning their lungs, the vets and trainers inject the horses with Lasix hours before they race, thinning their bones and breaking their legs. Deplorable ethics, no ethics at all. Horses don't need drugs to race, never have, never should."

This was not the first lecture Oberly had received over the dead by night, but it was the one he heard most often. Vallerone, knowing Blackfoot natural, was obsessed about the care of stabled horses. He'd become distraught at how drugs in the hands of horse doctors had come to replace horsemanship.

"Of all species, the horse is most holistically dependent." Vallerone held his arms over his head in a circle and turned 360°. "To keep horses healthy, natural has to be re-created in the stable. For a horse, health is movement. To walk is to breathe."

Spokane became Vallerone's poster child for his abundant-daily-locomotion lecture at the tribal college. What held in 1889 for horse health, held today.

"How can a Montana-bred born in 1886 grow up to win the Kentucky Derby halfway across the continent?" Oberly asked, wanting more. The two had the whole night to talk, the entire world theirs.

"Spokane foaled in Madison County, born of the range savvy mare Interpose...who, it was said by Fat Jack, ran off to join a wild band of horses to foal her baby Spokane, horses of Nez Perce and Palouse descent. Spokane learnt to win in this rogue band."

Oberly absorbed Vallerone's storytelling. It took him back to Heart Butte, to the medicine lodge tales. "Fascinating. You're telling me a horse foaled in frontier Montana journeyed from Madison County to Kentucky, and *win* the 1889 Kentucky Derby by a nostril?"

"It happened. Spokane was no fluke. He developed lung and leg through his Montana raising. He acquired the essential notion to win from the teachings of the wild ones. The wildest colt makes the gamest runner, you know."

Oberly knew. He listened.

"Conditioning for the Kentucky Derby relies on miles of daily walking. Spokane walked halfway to Kentucky to win the Derby. Beat Proctor Knot in the Clark Stakes in Louisville, went on to win the American Derby in Chicago, the Triple Crown of his time. He foiled the challengers every time. Eight hundred Palouse horses gave the runner soul. Spokane had the Indian sign on the Kentuckians. All horses have heart, but Spokane had soul, the spirit horse emerged from the eight hundred, sort of like you emerged from the Flood of '64, spirit of the lost."

Fingers' rapt voice intoned the night. His storytelling

resonated rhythm, a footfall cadence.

"Tell me more," Oberly requested, envisioning his emergence from the Flood of '64.

"Spokane is not so much a city in Washington State as the Indian word for the Child of the Sun. The Morning Star is the child of the Sun and Moon. Indians called the Morning Star 'Spokane.' Spokane, the child, the star child. Spokane, the salmon-eating inland Indians."

"Indians like their horses and stars," Oberly put in. "They like their wolves and salmon."

"The US Army had a long history of murdering Indian horses, an immoral military tactic. Murdered horses, like murdered Indians, rise out of the dust to prevail."

"The horse always has the last word," Oberly added.

"The Indian, as well."

"I don't know about that," Oberly said.

"Spokane's spirit to win the Kentucky Derby came about decades earlier. In 1858, to conquer the Palouse Indians, an army commander named Wright ordered the killing of all their captured horses. In one campaign, he had 800 horses shot dead. Most of the slayed horses belonged to Palouse Chief Tilcoax's tribe. In time, spirits arose from the murdered Indian horses. Their collective spirit gathered as horses gather, and waited for the right horse to come along. The spirits found the foal Spokane and settled into the game colt. That's how a Montana-bred wins the Kentucky Derby. The spirits of the eight hundred impelled Spokane."

"Wow."

"The ancestral band, the survivors, gave the foal soul, running the youngster hard and fast in close company over the Montana plains. They gave Spokane the confidence to run through and by swift horses. The band enlivened his spirit to persevere, to prevail, same as your ancestors spirited you to prevail. Spokane bested all the horses in America. What a runner. Such a beautiful runner!"

Oberly listened with pleasure, learning long ago to

listen to stories told by starlight. "All a century and a half or so ago, and at a mile and a half."

"Yes. Noah Armstrong bred Spokane to endure, to hold sway. He'd attended college in Canada, becoming a pharmacist. Not sure what that had to do with the victory, nothing, I'm thinking. Noah, knowing drugs, knew their danger with horses. Proctor Knot was said to be the hopped one.

"With that animal twinkle in his eye passed down from his forebears, Noah emigrated to America to take up cattle and horse ranching, a more natural commerce to his liking. He sashayed into Montana in the early 1880s behind enough cattle to feed the burgeoning gold rush population, toilers lured to the promise of Montana gold, hungry toilers. Miners cherish meat. They pay with gold on the barrelhead. Noah raised horses to tend cattle, deliver beef, and carry his gold back east. As wild meat became sparse—the sea of buffalo extinct by 1883—Noah delivered the beef."

"Indians don't care much for gold," Oberly emphasized. "The buffalo were our gold, our brethren."

"Gold is never good for natives. Noah could see that the gold in the ground would not last. The lasting gold was in the lush grass of the region. Noah knew to raise horses on this nutritious grass. The native forage delivered the calcium and phosphorus to build bone and flesh. He had a keen interest in thoroughbred racing, and he knew there were minerals richer than gold in the Montana grass, minerals that put leg into Spokane."

"How'd Spokane travel all the way from Montana to Kentucky? How'd that happen in the 1880s?"

"Early in his two-year-old year, Spokane and his trainer walked to Dillon, 40 miles to the south. After the long walk, they hopped a train to Memphis to enter track training. It was the spiriting in Montana and the hoofing from his birthplace to Dillon that put the lung into Spokane, the eight hundred breathing with him every step.

Noah raced the horse in Chicago before delivering the three-year-old to Louisville in the spring of 1889, fit as a Kentucky fiddle. What a bluegrass day!"

"As if you were there."

"Yes. The spirit is in me. The spirit is in you. La Corredera gives the spirit up to us, now: A sunny green day, a perfect track. A tough field of bluebloods. The Montana-bred ambled in to run down Proctor Knott, catching him under the wire in a lofty contest. As taught by the Indian herd, Spokane came off the pace to win the fable, the run for the roses. He set a record time that holds to this day, 2:34:1/2 for the mile and a half. Spokane spirited his way from Montana to Kentucky to win the classic of classics."

"Then what?"

"He stayed on for a while in Kentucky and bred mares, sired some winners. After his stud career, Noah brought Spokane home to Montana to live out his years, bringing the spirit of the eight hundred home. Spokane died in 1916, two years after Swift Dam began stopping the flow."

When Fingers' voice ceased trilling, Oberly resumed cranking. The two coerced La Corredera out of the borrow pit and into the peace and grass of a roadside meadow, night air warm as the dead horse. A gurgle of defiance percolated within the mare, indefinable, the horse's spirit fleeing its crumpled body to find another. "Takes a long time for a big animal to stop living, a long time for the strength to find its way home," Fingers explained.

"She's working the grass to fuel a run all the way to heaven," Oberly added, knowing how to put a horse to rest.

"Takes a bit of time for all the organs to get the message death has arrived."

"It is told some people talk after they're dead."

"Who told?" Vallerone asked.

"The Birch Creek clan. My people." The mare rumbled. Vallerone stood slack-jawed. "I thought you said horses

37

die quickly, that a quick death is their pain-escaping trait," Oberly put in.

"I did say that. I believe that."

"Death lingers over La Corredera."

"Tout le cheval est dans son intestin. The horse lives in her gut. The mare is dead, her guts stir; the spirit inside, deep inside. Horses are comfort seekers, safety seekers. Men, too. If there is no comfort, there can be no life. A horse's comfort comes from friends. To be with other horses is their safety."

"And here she died alone, looking for grass, green Montana grass, spirit grass. A car, a bullet, a gaff..." Oberly summarized.

Vallerone sang the Spokane song, a take on the Kentucky tune sung by the gambler Fat Jack, the player who followed Spokane to Memphis, on to Chicago, and then to the Kentucky Derby, the player who knew of the spirit, cashing big on the 16:1 winner, a wealthy man for a time.

There came from the Rockies
Faraway out West
A horse named Spokane
Of all runners, the best.

The most beautiful chestnut
Ever since seen
He came from Montana
Where bone grass grows green.

Spokane! Spokane!
Such a persevering flyer
You've returned to Montana
And take us all higher.

"His spirit remains in Montana. Spokane's spirit, the spirit of the eight hundred."

"Yes."

The men waited for sounds to cease, for the mare to stop speaking, for death to cool. But death would not cool, nor would the night. They stood listening.

It is peculiar what memories men remember, what horses and what women. Oberly remembered that horse well, the words Fingers shared in memory of the horse they brought home as best they could.

PAVLOV

*"H*ow long did you let your phone ring before you answered it?" he'd asked Fingers so long ago, speaking over the horse.

"A long time," Fingers said. "I like to see how determined the callers are. Polite people hang up after four or five rings if it's trouble that can wait, a hint of something brewing, perhaps. Others never hang up."

"Dispatch has their own code for me if I don't answer after six rings. They hang up and call back, let it ring twice, and then call again. That's how they get me on the line if I'm not apt to answer."

"That is a lot of ringing. I'll remember that," Vallerone replied.

Oberly knew Dr. Vallerone to be a student of Pavlov, dog doctor and all. Bird shared the Pavlov theory with Fingers. The veterinarian contemplated the Pavlovian notion of conditioned arousal with a torn-pocket smile. Middle of the Montana night, full moon, guardians of a dead horse, Pavlov. Wives at home in bed. Waiting.

In the years since Pavlov's belling was first suggested as conditioning their women for sexual delight, Fingers and

Bird tested their theory. In the aftermaths of nocturnal debacles and near-debacles, various aspects of their wives' sexual receptivity were explored after the ringing of their phones. When Bird's wife purchased a new landline with a different ring, everything had to be re-learned. Doc never let a new phone into his bedroom, sticking with the original dial-up with a real bell.

The men talked about their dogs as well as their wives, Pavlov and women, inquiries of importance to men of the night. Dogs kept both men company over the miles of moonlit road. Dogs and men, birds of a feather. All the virtues men wish to see in their fellow men they observe in their dogs. Of these noble canine qualities, Oberly and Vallerone contemplated and spoke. Fingers travelled with a cowdog, as did all ranchers up and down the Front. The most socialized cowdogs became the most versatile and content. The sheriff travelled with his border collie and a cadaver dog, a beagle with a nose for flesh. Dogs became a part of each man's professional life, the men becoming a part of their dogs. As time crept forward, a new dog periodically rejuvenated their lives. Dogs bestowed a helpful, essential rhythm to Oberly and Vallerone, company to tend the world at night.

Beyond dogs, the question arose as to whether to share their Pavlovian speculations with their wives. No, they decided. It could ruin everything; sexual fortune and confidence. The night might come when one might have to call the other, getting a ringing going in the cool darkness... So went their farce, a collective delusion, hope and science searching for something positive about phones ringing in the night.

Ivan Petrovich Pavlov, physiologist. Ring, ring, ring. Hey, hey, hey. A fine way to train the wife, drooling, wincing what their spouses might think about the concept. True, some women might embrace the phone fantasy, hoping for phone calls more than their husbands would ever know. The wives could just as easily despise the concept, making notions of Pavlov grounds for divorce. One never knew with women. It depended on a hundred different feelings sifted through a thousand different moods. Best not say a word to the wives; no, not while the phone still rang regular in the nights of their lives, and the love still followed. In the end, the sheriff and veterinarian were more victims of midnight ringings than they were beneficiaries. Their camaraderie matured through the decades, a silent distant understanding. Fingers was allowed to speed to bona fide veterinary emergencies. In return, Fingers took care of Bird's horses and dogs *pro bono*. An alliance developed, embellished by disparate ages and upbringings.

When Bird fielded earlier reports of Fingers' moondriving, two years back now, he found himself interested in a way he didn't fully understand. What was he really doing at Swift Dam? And what of the black bag? Oberly's mother lived just north of Swift Dam with Uncle Howler. She lived on the bench above Birch Creek, the family cow camp they'd inhabited above the river bottom after the Flood of '64. Shortly after losing her husband in the Flood, Oberly's mother married a friend of her dead husband's, a man named Harold Oberly, a Lummi Indian from the Straits of Juan de Fuca in the Puget Sound, a schoolteacher come to Heart Butte. The marriage did not last. The makeshift husband moved back to the coast shortly after Bird Oberly was born. Harold Oberly's last name was the only thing that remained with the boy.

Time crept in on the sheriff's mother as it crept in on Doc Vallerone, their bones hollowing like all bones. And now Fingers spending night after fullmoon night up her way. The practice and theory of moondriving. A big circular trip is what life was all about, Oberly thought. Watch the moon go round.

The phone rang again and Oberly didn't answer. No, he let it ring and ring and ring. His wife purred. He slid his hand over her furrowed ribcage, finding an attentive breast. He located the ring of pliant skin around her nipple, the goose bumps... The wife sighed. The sheriff hardened. His distracted mind reviewed Ricky's conversation on the phone, a reflective mindset taught him by the law enforcement academy, the school where he had had the only extramarital affair of his life, a female undersheriff down from the HiLine who initiated the whole shebang. Forget that. He loved his wife. He loved her nipples. He fondled them and loved everything about her. He fondled his guilt away.

Ricky's claim—that it was 'highly unusual' for his father to be gone all night—bothered Oberly. The son knew Fingers had missed plenty of nights at home through the years, and although the tenor of the missings may have changed, the absences continued, despite Ricky's denial. His dad's trips were periodic, and in most cases without apparent consequence. Fingers' wife of over half a century had even begun to tolerate his mysterious absences. The politics that interrupted the phone conversation resonated inside Oberly; the upcoming election, Ricky's comment about losing votes. It disturbed Oberly that the son had played a political card with his father gone missing, as if his missing father had anything to do with re-election. The black bag was what was missing.

Apparently, Ricky would never have realized his dad was missing had he not stopped by to visit his mother that evening. Maple had heard from the mayor that Fingers had emerged from the bank, black bag in tow. And furthermore, Bird discovered—inside his wife now, stroking, spooned perfectly behind her—that although the son knew his father had been MIA often enough, he evidently didn't know his father had taken to spending nights Swift Dam way, especially the last few years; news to the son perhaps, but not to Bird.

The sheriff had asked Ricky why he hadn't tracked down his dad himself. Bird pointed out that he could have headed his father off at the pass, rather than holding out until four in the morning to phone him. Most of the locals knew Doc Vallerone day-wise, the son included, but Sheriff Oberly understood Fingers night-wise, witness to his vulpine forays; not a Jekyll and Hyde exactly, but a man with crepuscular tendencies, a traveler of the full moon sort, a moondriver with a mission.

Bird and Fingers' paths crossed plenty still. Vallerone, fit as a fiddle in his old age seemed to appear everywhere, and often out of nowhere. If it wasn't a roadkill they helped along, it was Oberly holding down some grand theft auto roadblock as Fingers cruised in from the Big Open, clotted cesarean blood braiding the hair on the back of his forearms. Fingers was too high-strung these days to sleep after a night interrupted by field surgery. If the two met at night, they would visit until first light, the world at night offering a pleasant space for them to visit. They went over Pondera County politics, rumors and truths, stories of this and that, of him and her. Both men were storytelling buffs, many stories in their lines of work, lots to tell. Their dogs wrestled and ran as the rising sun cracked open another day under the Front Range.

Doctor Fingers had led quite a life, hard and honest work for decades, half the grind at night; the life of a cow and horse doctor in a land of cows and horses. First licensed vet in a hundred-mile radius, a man in his element, landless son of a horsetrader finding a niche on the reservation fringe. He shod horses through vet school, and landed along the Front after a stint with the thoroughbreds and standardbreds of New York, best horse doctor Montana ever harbored. Raised by horses, then back east to tend horses where they stood stabled in droves, he returned with a sense of the hand of man.

Fingers Vallerone worked Montana hard, memories of New York racehorses remaining with him. Fifty-some years later, he chased around the countryside still, relieving gravid cows and encephalitic horses. The new vets wanted the animals brought to town, and there they waited, no moondriving the countryside for them, no more animal ambulance services. Vallerone had spoiled his clients through the years, motoring to them at the spin of a dial. He catered to owners who knew better than to bring their livestock to the veterinary clinic, especially those willing to pay him for his time. A few of his recent clients traded grass for his services, grass to graze the small herd of cows he had gathered together, but securing grass to graze became a hit and miss prospect with drought and the like. Every other year or so, grass became scarce. It didn't rain like it used to rain.

LUCK

*E*very horse has his day, and a half century into his veterinary career, things changed for Doctor Vallerone. He long figured that someday an animal would connect him to something bigger than Conrad, how couldn't it be? All it would take would be one horse, or dog. He hoped it would be a racehorse, but it was a hunting dog.

A New York City literary agent walked into his clinic on a Sunday afternoon when he happened to be checking on a hospitalized cat that belonged to his favorite cat lady. The woman, outfitted in designer fly-fishing garb, carried a quilled dog in her arms. She walked through his door and introduced herself as Ms. Mardo Doherty, Mardo short for Margaret.

"I need some help. If you're the doctor, I feel blessed. I know it is Sunday, but this can't wait.'

"That's right," Vallerone replied. "A quilling is an emergency."

"I'm an agent from New York, visiting with my client, a mystery writer, a bird hunter."

"I see," said Vallerone. "You've caught me here, and I am happy to help."

The dog lifted his head from her arms to assess

47

Vallerone, a shamed look in his eye; no pheasant, this. He wagged his tail and Vallerone let him smell his wrist before rubbing the top of his head, one of the few spots without quills.

One might surmise upon looking at the pooch that the porcupine must be wandering about naked somewhere out there. It seemed that the griffon terrier had tried to consume the prickly critter, such an awful lot of quills, some deep in the face and neck, quills down the throat impaling the tongue. Additionally, unusual in porcupine quillings in Doc's experience, the dog had a number of quills in the groin area, as if he might have had the added indiscretion of trying to mate with the critter.

Fingers lifted a lip to assess the dog's gums and sensed the dog was slipping into circulatory shock; sensitive creatures, hi-bred terriers. Quillings can be fatal. Consoling the shivering creature, he lifted the pheasant-sniffer out of Mardo's arms. Continuing to pet the dog, he laid it out on the blanket covering his heated surgery table. After a time spent stroking the impaled griffon, the Conrad vet eased into a physical examination. He checked the hydration, pinching the skin over the shoulderblades, over the eyelid. Fingers listened to the wispy heart and struggling lungs with his ancient black-rubber stethoscope, his Littman. He clipped the leg vein with surgical scissors, and swabbed the skin. He tightened a temporary tourniquet and deftly slipped a catheter into the foreleg vein, seemingly all in one fluid motion that somehow hypnotized the usually high-strung hunting dog. The focused veterinarian started dripping some warm fluids into the dog, Fingers Vallerone the one-man-band of veterinary medicine. Once the fluid had dripped its magic, relaxing the dog and providing metabolic relief, the dog came to appreciate Dr. Vallerone.

Reaching into his pharmaceutical refrigerator, the veterinarian mixed and loaded and slipped Solu Delta Cortef™ into the dog's bloodstream, blending it with the electrolyte fluids, revitalizing the heavily-quilled dog. The same formula had saved many dogs and horses and cows and cats in Pondera County Montana. IV fluids and cortisone can turn tragedy around—cortisone, the tonic to resolve circulatory collapse, the drug that bolstered many a life in the hands of Fingers Vallerone. After the intravenous cortisone, Doc knocked some morphine into the quilled dog's vein, easing the pain and sending the dog into cattail heaven, followed by a low flow of antibiotics in the IV drip. He drew a tray of sterile water, added a squirt of blue disinfectant, and gathered his favorite set of quill removing forceps and needle-nosed tweezers.

With his patient narcotized, he began the meticulous process of removing quills, every quill. One missed quill was all it took to impale a heart. He first removed the quills slammed into the tissues of the nose and mouth and tongue, and then hooked the dog up to a flow of oxygen. Oxygen: Vallerone had learned to use oxygen as medicine through the decades. Oxygen helps heal nearly every condition.

There are strategies animal doctors acquire to remove quills in an effective and efficient fashion—practice they call it—a certain grasp, a special tug, a favored direction. Care is taken to not break off any quill, leaving the harpoon tip to travel to vital organs and joints. Time has to be set aside to perform the procedure without causing harm, or future harm. Veterinarians are not allowed to leave a quill or two, or portions of quills, as quills migrate, some lethally. Dog owners leave quills in their dogs, not veterinarians.

The owner of the dog, Mardo's murder-mystery novelist Riel Du Pré, became queasy at the sight of his impaled anesthetized pet. He stumbled out of the exam room to barf in the waiting room garbage can. The life of a veterinarian is many splendored, and like most veterinarians, the title is veterinarian/janitor, so it would be Vallerone cleaning up the puke. The agent held sway and stayed on to help, paling but intrigued by Dr. Fingers' finesse. The Sunday veterinarian turned up the oxygen and put the willing Mardo to work.

"If you insist on hanging around, grab that receptacle, please. Over in that drawer is a strainer. Could you bring it here, please, to dip the quills out of my water?"

Quills are hollow. They float. Indians use them for jewelry, the adornment of vests, headdresses, and moccasins. Vallerone saves quills for his Indian friends. Quills from porcupines still living are most desired.

To remove extracted quills from his instrument, he dips the instrument in the disinfectant water. A thousand puncture wounds disinfected. Mardo assisted as instructed, placing the extracted quills in a container to be delivered to the moccasin women. Certain quills had certain attributes, and the women prized Vallerone's quills. Man's dog has long harvested porcupine quills for Indians. Fresh quills are easiest to use, as they retain flexibility. Some dogs learn to avoid porcupines, but not all.

Before Vallerone fell in with the Indians, he had learned that quills wreak havoc on septic systems. The first and last batch of quills that Doc dumped down the drain resulted in an expensive drainfield replacement project. Quills bridged the percolation holes, and then the quills caught all the dog and cat hair clippings that Vallerone washed down the drain. The resulting textile plugged everything, and back came the sewer system. One thing a veterinarian tires of is fecal material. The day the human feces started backing into Vallerone's clinic was the day Vallerone set out upon what would be a long string of periodic disappearances. As a veterinarian, it was easy to come up with an alibi as to where one might have been, and why. As always, he explained that he was tending to the animals in need, just as he was doing on a Sunday for the griffon. Time is nothing to an animal.

As requested, Nurse Mardo daubed the tiny blooms of blood from the quill impalings with disinfectant sponges. As she did this, beads of sweat bloomed on her upper lip, sweat the Doctor noticed. He'd learned early in his career that the best way to avoid missing a quill was adequate lighting. A large, luminous, somewhat hot second-hand surgery light from the hospital lit his surgical field while heating Mardo's face. Doc kept her moving, knowing to keep those new to surgery busy. Removing quills wasn't neurosurgery, but certain quills sometimes had to be fished out with finesse. Stubborn impalements needed surgical scissors, or assistance from a tiny scalpel—careful not to cut a facial nerve, doctor. Quills half-way down the throat, quills in the flanks, in the abdomen. Mardo watched the doctor come into a rhythm with his patient—the anesthesia, the IV drip, the oxygen; Fingers' constant monitoring of vital signs, his intuitive quill extractions, the care so as not to break one off, or overlook even one.

The lit agent relished her experience with the veterinarian. In the claustrophobia of the surgical suite she felt dreamy, as if a character had come alive in one of the novels she represented. Mardo was in a story. The story felt fine, a human-helping-animal story, the story readers relish. For some reason unknown to her, perhaps to lessen the meticulous process of removing so many quills—an overwhelming number, really, the dog quilled from head to toe—she began telling the doctor her life story, how peddling fiction came to be her profession. Fingers listened as he de-quilled the dog.

The agent described how, as a child, she'd always dreamed of becoming a veterinarian. Three out of five people tell veterinarians they once planned to become a veterinarian themselves. They follow with their reasons for not making it into veterinary college: grades, love, marriage, vivisection, money, divorce. To be an animal doctor, you must get A's in college, not to mention steeling yourself to animal research and experimentation. Mardo explained that, in the end, she couldn't accept the animal tragedy involved in a veterinary education. She said she considered vet school in England, where a kinder, gentler animal world existed, a place where they educated veterinarians without performing unnecessary surgeries, where there were no euthanasias of convenience. Fingers nodded in agreement, listening as he watched the dog's respiration, dequilling, dequilling, surgically dequilling—precise, practiced hands. He listened and worked. Vivisection, euthanasia—Mardo pointing out the price one pays to heal.

Vallerone had discontinued performing euthanasia. He could no longer handle the task, leaving it to the younger associates when necessary, at times allowing pets to die in peace in their guardian's arms as the guardian would allow their human to pass, medicated or natural—guardian-assisted, rather than doctor-assisted. He arranged doctor-facilitated hospice, showed people the Indian way to move dogs and cats into the crossover. Vallerone came to be known as the graceful-aging specialist. Meat, he prescribed raw meat be fed to aging dogs, raw meat and bones, and the dogs flourished.

Mardo displayed the usual awe at his veterinary insight—how rewarding it must be to resolve troubles for the aging, or troubles such as this poor griffon's. She explained how she was on a book tour with her client, how he'd had to go bird hunting with the natives, and how embarrassing it was when his dog attacked the porcupine, a sacred animal to the author's characters, the Métis.

Doc nodded, and requested a change of disinfectant water. Doc knew porcupines as sacred wildlife. They maintained their sacred space with their sacred quills, a boundary honored by fox and wolf, but not dog, most dogs, but not all. Vallerone's dogs knew to avoid porcupine.

Mardo changed the water and rinsed his instruments of blood. After a period of silence, Doc asked her the secret to the agenting business. "What is required to sell a novel to a publishing house, to cash a check?"

"Locution, locution, locution," she said.

"The author or the agent?" Fingers asked.

"Both, as it turns out."

"Isn't that a line from a Richard Ford novel?"

"You are well read."

"Richard wrote the novel in Chinook, just down the Hi-line."

"That Big Open seems a fine place to write a novel."

"The finest."

Fingers considered the story he'd composed, years stringing words together, creating and disassembling sentences, changing their order...deletion, deletion. Rewrites. Edits. Revisions and excisions. Surgery. Making sentences smooth, read-aloud smooth. He'd heard tell of literary agents and their car-salesman nature, and had queried some. Now one stood before him; he with the finished story in hand.

As Doc dequilled, he considered publication, his heart beating high in his chest, a happy beat. He could feel the blood swinging through his aorta, centripetal, centrifugal, a primal sensation previously experienced only after strenuous exercise or novel sex. Doc looked up at his impromptu assistant. He dreamt of readers. The surgical illumination lit her as an angel, a literary savior. Vallerone came to feel as if he was in a dream, a book and a man and a woman and a dog, dreaming together. Which side of the dream, which side now?

He laughed: dog in the domestication dance with man having commandeered mankind to provide emergency medical services. He provided dog with those services; modern, compassionate, humane, effective and efficient. Painless. The three lived on, dog breathing unconsciously, quills coming out, pools of blood daubed away. Agent, author, dog. Blood, quills and blood. Space. Sacred space.

Every so often Mardo licked the beads of sweat from her upper lip—delicate, discreet swipes with her tongue. Vallerone, not lost on her motion, watched her savor the taste of her salt. She sometimes licked when she caught the doctor looking in her eyes. Hundreds of quills, maybe thousands, two hours worth of quills, extractions followed by a bloom of blood daubed by the agent. Beads of sweat and blood. Ever so often, Vallerone would close the dog's eyelids over his corneas to wet them, taking care to keep the eyes moist and healthy. In time, Mardo stopped talking. Vallerone schemed. Like most people telling veterinarians that they always wanted to become one, most agents probably heard from three out of five people that they had written a novel, and would they please consider representing the book.

"I write a bit," he mentioned. "Stories in Montana slicks."

"Fiction?"

"Well, you know. Yes."

"What magazines?" she asked, smiling.

"*Montana Quarterly.*"

"A recent story?"

"Yes, just published. I like people reading my stuff."

"The latest issue?"

"Yes, the current edition, I believe."

"The piece entitled *'smallpox'?*"

"That's my story."

"I read the story. A fine story."

Rather than speed up, his heart rate relaxed, as if his heart had been waiting for a storytelling compliment from someone who mattered. The agent closed her eyes, hung her head, and rubbed the corner of her neck taken back into the story she'd read the day before, his story.

"Have you written a novel?"

"Yes."

As the dequilling neared completion, Fingers shared a brief synopsis of his novel with her. "A novel of regeneration, of miscegenation. Manifest Destiny..."

"Miscegenation?"

"The blending of peoples, of time. Of people, time, and land."

"And animals?"

"Yes, the merger, the blending of animal society with human; the un-blending."

"Indians?"

"Blackfeet Indians."

"Blackfeet or Blackfoot?"

"Pikunni, they call themselves Pikunni and other names. Their business. Who are we to name them? They are resurrecting their Blackfeet language, you know. Napi lives."

The agent, impressed as much by his magazine yarn as his finesse with the dog, contemplated Fingers' explanation of his novel. To read a written query was one thing, to listen to the writer's explanation, another.

"I'll give it a read."

The two finished removing the quills in silence. Give it a read, Vallerone thought, give it a read. It.

When no quills remained, Fingers palpated the dog from nose to tail, circumferentially, tail to toe and between pads, through the biological maze of *Canis lupus familiaris*, no nook of the friend of man left unfelt. Quills unseen are quills felt—a thorough massage as exploratory exam. The doctor found three more quills, fishing them surgically from underneath the skin. Instruments in the hands of a practiced surgeon travel in the most fascinating patterns. The moves one makes as a practicing veterinary surgeon impressed Mardo. Satisfied, Vallerone unhooked the oxygen, wonderful stuff that oxygen. He transferred the dog to the heated recovery area to infuse another warmed bag of intravenous fluids. "I'd like to keep your terrier overnight."

"Du Pré's terrier..."

"It seems you are the guardian." Vallerone adjusted the dog into sternal recumbancy in the recovery cage, checking the vital signs. He ascertained the dog's temperature with the ear sensor the new doctors purchased. "He's a little cool, not all bad. Seems to minimize over-reactivity." The veterinarian hovered over the wirehair, positioning a heating pad under the dog, continuing with a thorough massage, the veterinarian taking full advantage of opportunities presented. Practice, the practiced doctor of veterinary medicine.

"We'll meet tomorrow," he suggested. "I have your cell. No news is good news."

"Is anyone going to stay with the dog?"

"I'll stay until I know he is out from under my anesthesia. I usually stay with them until they can chew a raw bone."

"And you always know?"

"Know what?"

"If an animal is to live or to die?"

"No, not always, mostly, but never always. No, always is not a word we use in veterinary medicine, always or never."

"Honest enough."

"I have learned when to let sleeping dogs lie, when to get out of their way, to leave them to heal as they are born to heal," he offered. Infallible, Vallerone thought—she does not believe I am infallible when it comes to healing. She's not the first, he smiled.

"You must have lost some patients. Some deaths must have come as surprises."

"I've learnt what not to do. If that's what you mean."

"Both in action and word, I presume."

Vallerone liked this agent. He had a notion she would admire *Horses*. "I have had a fair amount of practice. You can't play this veterinary game in these parts without learning. One tries to avoid surprises when it comes to life and death. No doctor likes to make that phone call informing the guardian of their pet's passage. I avoid that like the plague."

"Yes... of course."

"Actually, a pre-vet student lives in the apartment below. She'll be with your dog all night. But sometimes, as

I said, it is best to let sleepers sleep. She will be the first to know if any complications arise. I'll be the second. You'll be the third, and Du Pré, the fourth. That's how medicine works these days."

The dog lifted his head and looked up at the agent, and then at the doctor. The griffon blinked an eye, confirming Vallerone's favorable prognosis.

Mardo felt her blood bubble. Animal doctoring makes people quiver. In absorbing Vallerone's animal world—the willing alignment with his patient—she shuddered. She hoped these poses appeared in his novel. Du Pré's dog lived, saved by Vallerone. The dog would heal and all will be well, save an overlooked quill. When the dog first appeared, the condition appeared fatal.

Vallerone saved a life, setting the tone for Mardo to like his novel. Much of what an agent feels about a manuscript is dependent on the agent's mood at the time of her reading. Vallerone did his best to put her in a mood, the nurturer mood, a mislaid mood awaited by the animal readers of the world—the merging of writer and doctor, the knitting of animals into the dilemmas of men and women.

"Thanks for all your help." She gathered her bag and departed to find her client whom Fingers had sent to the Lariat Tavern to commune with the local sons of the soil, the farmers of pheasants, the place serving up bromides of all sorts.

Fingers left the dog in peace, all alone with his raw bone. Take away the animal's pain, remove the quills of living, give the dog a bone, and he heals. He left the vet-student a note to check on the dog. He walked home, a nimble cadence. Life-saving efforts sustained his psyche. The hope for his novel.

He arrived, wished Maple her evening happiness, and marched to his den and printed out his creation, words to heal the world. He savored the hitching sound of the ancient printer ratcheting out the story in black and white.

Readers could picture his black and white world any color they wanted. What made humans different than animals were words, printed words creating imagined lives, lives the readers' imagined as their lives might be, or would be; could be.

He read the printed pages—all night, he read. He edited, first on paper, then on the word processor. He took sentences out, retooled paragraphs, and finished what he estimated to be his final revision. Satisfied there weren't any quills left in the manuscript to impale an editor outright, he re-printed the manuscript, handling and ordering and stacking the pages on his kitchen table, Maple drinking her tea, watching her life mate perform the sacred act of printing the version for delivery, the version that would go from a stack of paper to a hard bound book. He picked up the ordered manuscript, liking its heft. He rapped the edges on the table, aligning the four sides into a smooth rectangle. He offered goodnight to Maple, and slipped off to sleep one of the deeper sleeps of this life.

Mardo showed up the next morning to retrieve the griffon. The dog bounded out of Dr. Vallerone's establishment as if nothing had happened, ducking and diving, sniffing a big loop around the hospital, marking the fire hydrant and rose bushes, sneezing and barking. Fingers had his manuscript boxed and waiting on the counter. Mardo collared the dog, and set her shoulder bag next to his pages.

"Your fee?" Mardo asked.

Fingers balked, eyeing his boxed manuscript.

"Business is business," she said, shuffling though a pocket to retrieve a wallet. She handed him an Amex card. Vallerone ran the sale; a credit card swiped, the ratcheting of a receipt, a ratcheting not unlike the printing of his manuscript. Money turns the world, money and stitches, and soon—words.

She signed the receipt, refused her copy, and tapped

the boxed manuscript with her index fingernail.

"That's it. My life's work," he said.

Grasping the boxed manuscript with slender fingers, she placed Vallerone's *opus* into her bag, most gracious move by a woman Vallerone had witnessed in some time, the slinging of his words over her shoulder. She snapped away the credit card, knowing Vallerone saw it was hers. "Not my money. Du Pré's." She gestured outside, money meant little to a writer. "I get fifteen percent of earnings and advances, deducting expenses, like this, say. Same arrangement you and I would have if this melts me." She squeezed the manuscript with her elbow.

"Whatever's standard," Vallerone responded, puffing, putting the receipts in the drawer for the staff to sort out.

"Fine, okay," Mardo replied, grabbing and squeezing his hand, a handshake, a Madison Avenue contract sealed Montana style. The heat in her fingers gave Vallerone hope. He wanted to say something regarding her consideration of his story, but could say nothing at all.

MEDICINE

Since the onset of irrigation, veterinary practice has flourished in Pondera County Montana. The water flowing in ditches dug with hydraulically engineered precision allows the sons of the soil to push the domesticates together, oh so close together.

Confinement farming, a practice abetted by irrigation, water making the land a land of fodder aplenty. Closer and closer they grew, resources spread thin, and thinner. Moving away from natural, their animals sickened, oh did they sicken. Vallerone came to know sickness. The veterinary practice came to treat non-stop ailments. More treatment with more and more drugs incited troubles on an epidemiologic scale—pathogen virulence, antibiotic resistance. Endemics, pandemics. Anaplasmosis, Brucellosis, shipping fever, milk fever. Infertility, dystocia, wooden tongue. Scours, pneumonia, brisket disease, hardware disease. Coccidiosis, helminthiasis, trichomoniasis. Blood worm, pin worm, round worm, tape. Bankrupt worm. *Clostridia, Salmonella, E. coli. Spherophorus necrophorus.*

Veterinary medicine flourished, Vallerone the

beneficiary of manifest malaise. Drugs and vaccines became management scrims to cut corners of inadequate husbandry. The more drugs required, the lower the animal welfare. The veterinary clinic became more dispensary than surgery, the doctors more pharmacist than physician. As progress overwhelmed agribusiness, and as agribusiness overwrought health, Doctor V became both anxious and reluctant to leave his practice in new hands. The more acquired knowledge he shared with his new veterinarians, the more he realized he would not be able to teach all they needed to know. The new docs had been taught using machines rather than fingers to diagnose and treat. They arrived pharmaceutically alienated, as if drugs and vaccination sheltered the demise of domestication. He persisted, stepping in a day or two each week, demonstrating his finesse with cats, for what can a doctor do with a cat that cannot be handled? He could train most any dog to submit to examination in a minute, all this when they were supposed to be reviewing financials and profit margins.

The new veterinarians felt they knew enough about dogs and cats, and did. They were hoping Vallerone limited his instruction to horses and cows. But no, the veterinary lessons continued inside and out, covering all domestic species that might wander through the door. Wildlife. Exotics. He'd done his share of birds, rehabbing corvids as conservancy. Raven doctor Vallerone developed a talent for pinning the fractured wing bones of ravens, wings fractured by gunshots, careless ravens. Vallerone considered it a sin to shoot a raven, relative of the mockingbird. "They chatter, showing the way. Ravens fly their hearts out for you. It is a sin to kill a raven."

Vallerone schooled the new doctors despite their resistance. It was his veterinary practice to sell, and sold it he did, demonstrating goodwill around patients and clients, calming the guardians to facilitate gentle handling of their faithful friends. He elucidated how an animal can see fear, how animals anticipate their handler's very thoughts by the handler's manner of action. He showed how to tone one's actions, to talk dog, horse, and cat, to gesture empathetic. He demonstrated the countenance reflected nobly in the eyes of horses. He taught by example. His patients acknowledged his help, this for all to see. The new doctors conceded that Vallerone had the touch, but they felt he'd fallen out of step with progress. He used penicillin, for example. And worse, cortisone, Dr. Triamcinolone himself, but justly so in his hands. To diagnose, the new doctors required data gleaned from machines of all things, digital imagery and blood chemistries. No longer was medicine an art drawn through physical examination. No longer were fingers important, all intuition set aside.

Despite this, Vallerone aired his healing confidence for all to witness, motions and gestures animals relished. He used his mind and body to diagnose and heal. Machines would not misguide Vallerone. Just how he approached a patient is difficult to explain, something read by those more animal than human. Experience shaped Vallerone's gestures. Open to learning from animals, he thrived amongst them. Animals trained the man to move as they expected him to move. He listened. He spoke their language.

To heal a herd animal one joins the herd. Group survivalists evolved to appreciate leaders moving with them, rather than against. All body actions convey information to animals. Animals talk to one another utilizing kinetic empathy, movement with meaning and conveyance, a body language Vallerone spoke fluently. As with their own, domestic animals sense people's intentions by assessing their moves. Vallerone became a bearer of good intentions in animal eyes. Vallerone danced with animals—leading, following, moving with them, motions emulated, soft movements, a gesture language. The more fluent the moves, the more efficient the healing.

Even though Vallerone had built the young doctors a

modern hospital, he prescribed sending patients home as soon as possible. Home is the place to heal. Animals crave familiar. All social species appreciate familiar—familiar friends, familiar surroundings. Cages are difficult places for animals sense comfort and security. Patients thrive on tender loving care, the most tender care at home. To heal, horses need other horses with them, at least one other. If you have to hospitalize a horse, make sure you find a compatible horse to keep the healing horse company. A pair-bonded horse from home is the best facilitator of healing, and any horse is better than no horse at all. The last place a horse evolved to thrive is alone in a stall in a veterinary clinic.

Vallerone assured the new veterinarians he would be available whenever they needed him. "Happy to do any cow and horse work wherever under the Front," he boasted. They complied. After a good dose of Vallerone's advice and insight, the new doctors felt that the less he might be around, the better. They handed him every faraway call, as intended. After a couple months of trying to pass off his knowledge, he appreciated his time to step aside had arrived.

Oh, the rags of growing old. He embraced change, driving into his veterinary afterlife. The setup succeeded. The hospital practice thrived without him. His wife hired an office manager and another doctor. Maple opened negotiations to sell the business. Soon, they no longer needed his assistance or wanted his guidance. No one is indispensable.

Meanwhile, Fingers kept in touch with his clients in the netherworld reaches of the Front. He enlarged his small herd of cattle a cow at a time. He purchased a new truck and aluminum trailer to pull his horses up and down the Front to tend his roving grazers. He bred and trained his thoroughbreds at Howler and Tess' Birch Creek bottom, and continued to do vet work for a select group of ranchers—reservation Indians, cowmen with grass. They kept him in his veterinary element, sheltering his cows on the good grass.

Like his rancher friends, Vallerone longed for permanence, a spread of his own, but after all his time with the Indians, fifty years contemplating Swift Dam, he'd become leery of land ownership. Like so many Indians he knew, Fingers entertained the thought—or is it a religion?—of owning nothing, and beyond that, having no need to own anything, the land belonging to all.

He treasured moving herd up and down the front, life as a gypsy cowboy, a wanderer the likes of ancient animal folk. Vallerone's cows savored their nomadic grass. His charges grazed fresh and rested grass, pastures that most ranchers couldn't get to; isolated sections, private Indian leases, under-grazed Forest Service allotments, and the backwater like. Fingers enjoyed the impermanence, the ability to wander, finding contentment amidst grass, as close to the life of ancients as one could get. Indian kids spent the summer weeks riding herd with him, days on end tending grazers. He enjoyed riding alongside the little horsemen, teaching them, learning from them, preparing them the freshest foods, picking the berries of their ancestors, cooking the native roots, smudging the sweetgrass. Fingers became impressed with their Indian horsemanship. They loved riding his bloodhorses. When the kids rode herd, he had not a care in the world, excepting maybe bears. The grizzlies had ventured to the prairies in recent years. Vallerone welcomed their return, giving predators their way, wolves likewise. The orders were to retreat whenever bears were sighted. He came to appreciate that the bears seldom bothered tended herds. As long as Vallerone rode herd, the wolves and bears kept their distance, sauntering by, moving on to shepherd less-shepherded flocks.

THE STORYTELLER

Mardo began reading the manuscript on the flight home. At times, she would look up from a page to stare out the airplane window. Her mystery writer slept beside her, exhausted from traipsing around Montana. The first chapter didn't fit her notion of what might sell. She imagined what the horse and hound doctor might be capable of telling. By chapter three she fell into the story, astonished by the crafted prose. With each following chapter, the doctor galvanized her belief in the story. She considered herself not one to be easily drawn in, but his rhythm had her.

Upon arriving in New York City, she had a literary associate case the story. She thought her fervor with the manuscript might be infatuation with Fingers, the way he'd handled the dog, the way he'd handled her as his assistant, and the method in which he introduced himself as a writer as he dequilled the Grif—this demeanor he had around animal and animal guardian, his bedside manner. She had the terrier's owner read the novel. Fingers' storytelling was unique, a story within the realm of possibilities.

A week later, after re-reading and formulating a pitch,

Mardo phoned Fingers in Conrad from her Madison Avenue office to let him know.

"Hello, Dr. Vallerone."

"Hi," he answered.

"I love *Horses.*"

"Horses? Yes, of course you do."

"Your novel, *Horses.* I'd like to represent the work, a real work of art for a doctor, a veterinarian no less. Seems that you are the only veterinarian in America to write a novel, literary fiction at any rate. I don't say 'work of art' about many of the books I represent."

"Why, thank you."

"That said, a work of art is sometimes harder to sell than a mystery or thriller, you know. Even harder than po-mo."

"Po-mo?" Doc asked.

"Post modern," she said.

"Oh, yes," he managed, in a state of suspension. "Is this the call, then, that novelists wait for?"

"Yes," she laughed, "Yes, this is that call, the first call anyways. Hopefully not the last."

"How so?"

"Your novel will be published if I find the right publisher. Two editors I'm close to expressed interest when I teased them with the veterinary lore. I am not certain, of course, but I don't think I will have much trouble bringing this into print. A decent advance is the question. Debut novels dubbed literary sometimes don't command a grand advance. It's a risky business, debut literary novels."

"You'll handle all the publication details, then?"

"Oh, yes. You'll have to approve and sign the contract in the end. You have final say."

"I appreciate your belief in the writing."

"Yes, well, now I have to make a publisher believe in it. We'll celebrate when that happens. In the meantime, write me another."

"Yes, of course."

"Beware of fame, or dreams of fame. Fame can lead to places hollow."

Fingers felt his heart beat, strong and slow. Best phone call he'd ever fielded, best in recent times. Talk about positive reinforcement. I'd like to represent that novel, the one you groveled over for a couple of decades. Oh, the marvel.

It had been some time since someone had called to tell him they believed. He was thrilled at his fortune. Porcupine had long been his totem. It takes time to appreciate one's helper, to know your spirit animal. Porcupine delivers, giving Vallerone a sacred space to live, a space beyond his veterinary life.

Two months later, Mardo sealed a deal, forwarding Fingers a $170,000 dollar advance, keeping $30,000 as commission. Biggest chunk of change Vallerone had ever handled at one time, but not the biggest he would ever handle if she had her way with the movie rights, which she claimed some had their sights on. Everyone loves a horse story. Fingers felt a certain relief, as if publication might validate his existence, ease the pain of time past, make the way for a progressive future. He wasn't certain about a movie. Serious writers wanted their novel protected, unblemished by Hollywood. Horses are difficult to portray.

Vallerone aspired for the world to know his horsemen, a life lived atop equus, the blending of horse and human. He wanted his readers drawn into the centaur culture *after* the buffalo. The book sold back East, and as such, the locals were forced to read the thing. His success was no fluke. Doc had been a lifelong reader, a reader of fiction. The Russians. Flaubert, Halldór Laxness, the Nobels, the twentieth century Americans, the war fictions, the revolutionary tales, the beats, New Yorker weekly, poetry up through Sherman Alexie, Cormac McCarthy's early fiction, and David Foster Wallace's last. Cervantes.

He read novels by night and plied the veterinary trade by day. Insomnia ran deep in the veterinarian's veins, reading the best soma of all. Through decades of mending animals under the Chinook Arch, he accommodated his fancy to write, an obsession festering since the Flood of '64. Off and on for decades he wrote. His wife and sons felt him touched by his marathon veterinary ministrations, an acquired neurosis from resolving relentless animal dealings at the hand of man. From time to time, from season to season, Dr. Vallerone locked himself away for a week at a time, not answering the phone, unable to separate his life from his writing.

He put the original *Horses* story down in a burst of creativity stored in the diverticula of his gray matter, the story building inside him through the years, formed of his meditations driving the countryside. He composed the first draft in four months, and had in-hand the basic tale, but he was no Faulkner, and many sentences were not right. He spent years crafting the narrative, days spent on a single digression, hours styling sentences and slimming dialog; seasons spent ruminating over a single word. Meanwhile, he submitted short stories and poems, vignettes and animal health ditties. Ever perseverant, little magazines started publishing his work, some paying him.

He considered realism and minimalism, embellishment and digression. He drove the countryside, spinning stories to fit the spooling landscape. Aloud, he conjured dialogue, reciting his poetry to his dog, crafting words to the ear, his ear. He stole idioms from his clients and dressed his characters like their hired help. In spells, when exhaustion had overtaken his body and mind—surgeries performed and yet to be performed—he hyped himself on the amphetamine sulphate he used to revive comatose calves. A drop or two brought a calf to life, and could keep Vallerone cutting all night long.

Mankind had missed the mark with exotic cattle breeding, but the legend drugs performed. Caesareans became the order of ranching in the 60s, a sorry genetic misjudgment that lingered in the phenotype for decades. To be a cow doctor was to Caesar heifers. Our surgeon of cows would return home pharmaceutically galvanized, clear minded and clairvoyant. He squeezed oranges, concocting a mineral water juice, drinking to flush his system to deliver the words. The stitcher of horseflesh sat at his desk to type his tale, to type and edit and retype, his cesarean insomnias useful and productive. He constructed and deconstructed, arranged and rearranged, embroidered, simplified, and excised. He let the manuscript cure. He re-read and deleted, struck adverbs. Slept and dreamt and travelled the countryside treating all creatures great and small, a veritable Herriot if ever there was one.

When Maple cased his introspective habits and unexplained absences, Fingers invited her to join his *novel* endeavor. He encouraged her to read his chapters aloud, to make novel writing a family affair. She agreed, having no choice. The other choice was to leave him to his solitary pursuit. Maple read aloud for him. The writer would close his eyes and listen, lips smiling and curling, mind whirling, ears reaching to refine the rhythm. Sometimes he talked his boys into reading a page or two for him. Hearing his boys read his words aloud became the pleasure of his life, although not theirs. The time came when neither boy would read his words to him. Fingers had failed to reward his readers. They would read to him. He would listen, only to run off without a moment's notice to hammer keys. The snapping electric typewriter spelled family loneliness as he fluttered his story away.

Maple stopped reading, or stopped reading with the enthusiasm necessary for Fingers to listen and revise. He took to reading his sentences aloud to himself. The act did not appeal to him anymore than it had to Maple, Harry, or Ricky. Like many writers, he took to reading and retooling his sentences in silence, an internal voice arising within his chest to whisper the paragraphs into his skull. His doppelgänger ordered and re-ordered the words, settling existential thoughts into neat sentences, or trying to.

Like an Icelandic poet, Fingers juggled words and phrases and sentences in his word-loving mind until they tumbled together in the correct order. He carried a notebook everywhere he travelled, never letting a notion escape his grasp. He had notebooks in his car, on his bedstead, and at his office. He left one at Howler's cow camp, the notebook Howler started reading, and later writing in.

Storytelling became Fingers' passion. He'd stop and write a story whenever or wherever the urge took him. He listened to stories on tapes—the old Indian woman from Charlo telling the story of how the skeleton became a skeleton. He listened to the tales his animal folk told, the best stories of all, Blackfeet lodge tales. Books on tape, public radio, Canadian radio. Sixty thousand miles of stories a year heard. A certain sense of worldly appreciation accompanied a story well told, his or whomever's.

More revisions. Deletion of adverbs, all adverbs; adjective refinement. Stronger nouns and verbs. Nouns as verbs. Movement in paragraphs. Active voice. Reworking, retooling. Narrative momentum. Inserting a rare adverb, an adjective; the right word! More deletion. Feedback. Copy edits. Line edits. Editing sessions with the Catholic.

Vallerone and his force of word-crafters labored to assure the language fit the story, that the characters did the storytelling. Of course he failed, all novelists fail. He polished sentences and streamlined the storytelling, or tried. He read books, novels both classic and contemporary, local and foreign, Midwest blear. Reading and revising, crafting, re-crafting, uncrafting. Letting words flow. Finding the zone.

After his novel became finalized for publication, after all the line edits and copyedits, Fingers continued to fiddle with the words, attempting to make the storytelling resonant. His wife knew how hard and long he had labored to get the words in the right order. Harry and Ricky knew. They knew writing as his vice to escape his veterinary travails. Both words and animals left them fatherless for weeks on end. They were not the beneficiaries of his endless narrative rewording and restructuring, but the novel's readers were.

Sheriff Oberly read the novel in its primal state. Admiring Fingers' oral tradition before he read the book, he became further connected afterwards, offering countless editing suggestions regarding Indians and horses, which made all the difference. Fingers' compassion for Bird's Indian kin was astounding. Bird honed the author's keen perception of the Indian plight. Indeed, a story well told, a stunning exploration of existence. The earth theme beautifully understated, the thread of animal domestication, the relationship of man to his natural surroundings, the coevolution of man and animal. The novel inspired Oberly, a reflection of man's endless struggle through time, a contemporary resonance no matter one's origins.

Vallerone wrote to make the world a better place, or that's why he thought he wrote his story—what he told himself. His poetic investigation of existence under the Front pleased him, published or unpublished. The process, the writing process engaged him with life. Manifestly, some of the story's romances rubbed too close to home. His portrayal of Pondera County's social fabric frayed the community's tolerance for scrutiny, their preference being he stick to veterinary medicine.

Like a horse, Vallerone began working for only those ranchers who appreciated him, those with a hand considerate as his. He stuck tight with the natural folk, and abandoned the pharmaceutical. He enjoyed working for the Indian ranchers, reveling his role as medicine man. He grazed his growing herd of cattle on finer and finer grass. New cows came his way each year in payment, cows he'd cured or mended, perhaps a calf delivered, later grown, warts and all.

Fingers spent more time up North with his travelling herd of cows and calves. He rode herd with the Indians, refuge from a life of stitching. He established a grub line for himself *and* his herd, and began holing up at Howler's high country summer cow camp for weeks at a time, bringing his remuda of horses along. He travelled horseback across the foothills with Many White Horses and his travois children. The Pondera Panhandle sheltered him.

RECAPITULATION

Vallerone recapitulates life. The elderly recall the past, the point being to live life fully young. The past is full of pain and joy, and the key becomes to let go of the bad to enjoy the ecstasies and epiphanies. He recalled the gored horse at the Lazy J he'd spent all night sewing up; how it died anyway, a week dark with disappointment. He retraced a long drive east to a heifer in trouble at the IX ranch, saving both her and her calf, a snowmoon cesarean most rewarding, the calf nursing the cudding heifer before he left, all the world healthy. Failures held more sway in the mind than successes, and Vallerone sought to remedy that. He began rethinking all his successes, all the creatures resurrected.

Nothing vague about the purpose of those bygone journeys, Fingers sliding his three-speed Impala over the rutty roads of the new frontier, cattle and grain having replaced the wild buffalo and nature-savvy Indians. He bemoaned how modern cattlemen had mucked up everything by pushing calving back into January and February, how the resulting confinement caused sickness. Sub-zero cesareans took the fun out of animal husbandry.

Drugs smothered the true cowman's life and derailed welfare.

As moons held Indian life together, moons kept Vallerone in one piece. Luna, his sister of the night, most nights, and if not her, her stars. When Luna hid behind the world, the stars did sparkle. New moon, full moon, Vallerone treasured all moons. He delighted in moonrises and moonsets. Travelling through the Sweetgrass Hills, Dr. Alphonse 'Fingers' Vallerone could experience two moonrises with the right kind of driving. The first moon rises from the high tableland, shining over the Great Plains of America. He drops into a coulee to witness a second moonrise snaking over a Marias River ridge—a moon twice risen.

A man of the night comes to feel the moon, to appreciate the moon, knowing her cycles as the animal cycles. The moon takes care of men of the night in a way the sun cares by day. Vallerone's recent trips became not so much drives to certain places, but returns to rejuvenated landscapes of the mind. He drives to relive and relieve time, to smell the night, feel the night, but most of all, to see the night. He drives under the moon. His memory speaks. Movement into the Big Open takes him back. Night travel submerges Alphonse into his dwindling past—unrequited, unreconciled.

A sight, a smell, a planet; any past image could launch the past forward, moments juggling time. The centrifugal sway of particular curves aroused feelings, memories repressed by worry and time. The silhouette of a barn, a sudden change in light, a certain sleet or hail could resurrect the past for Vallerone. Specific smells, precise swamps, swathed hay waiting to be baled, peculiar times of day or night, native bugs and birds. Rabbits and rodents. Hawks, eagles, grouse. Fingers drives and remembers, his memory alive with association. He becomes the night, driving until he cannot keep his eyes open.

Fingers Vallerone travels to a tiny ranch north of Swift

Dam, journeying back to a point in time long ago, five decades and a week ago, eighty-four miles of gravel road to find a hidden ranch. The light of a dim flashlight dances, a light guided by Howler Ground Owl and his sister Tess and her husband Ivan Buffalo Heart. The Indians walk through the world at night, leading the way to the animal trouble Ivan could not resolve. Howler and Tess lead Fingers into the homefield to their animal in trouble. Ivan Buffalo Heart follows, singing.

Fingers' headlight reveals a heifer sprawled at the bottom of a rain-washed gully, her calf waiting impatiently in the bottom of her belly, a baby trapped under all four stomachs, too big to exit the pelvis. Doc halters the heifer, gently securing her, preparing the servant of man for the scalpel of man, a new development in the coevolutionary domestication process, one Ivan found hard to accept. Vallerone operates under the scrutiny of stars as he would operate for decades to come. He looks up to Howler Ground Owl and Tess Buffalo Heart. He smiles at the Indians, wondering what they may be thinking, and prepares to perform surgery. Ivan waits in the dark.

Fingers Vallerone clips the hair with a hand tool. He washes the belly with disinfectant, the antiseptic smell crisping the mountain air. The needle man blocks the belly with Novocain. He scrubs his hands and arms, and brings forth the scalpel from the tray of sterile tools. He slices the skin deftly, his fingers guiding the scalpel to open the heifer up. He nimbly dissects with scissors and parts layers of muscle with his surgical fingers to enter the abdominal cavity. He pokes the peritoneum, the pristine membrane lining the abdomen, and whiffs the innard air.

A slice-of-ice moon laughs, the wind hums... Tess and Howler watch in wonder.

Alphonse takes a breath of the starry air. He guides his learning and learned fingers deep into the abdomen and locates the uterus. He rolls the womb into his surgical field with his left hand, and with his right opens the uterus with his scalpel. He snips blunt-blunt scissors to extend the incision to open the womb, scissoring in symphony with the muscle striations. A hind hoof pops through the uterus, placenta bound. Another hoof. Fingers peels the gelatinous placenta away, scissors snipping. He loops obstetric straps over the feet and with the help of Ivan Buffalo Heart extracts the calf from inside the heifer, delivering life where life could not before be delivered, the Indian's first calf by cesarean section, a miracle of modern veterinary medicine, the surgery cure.

The new mother heaves a sigh of relief as the calf exits her incised womb. Doc elevates the calf to drain her wet lungs, and lays the neonate out and revives the baby, too long inside. He clamps her umbilicus to make her inhale, and inhale the little creature does, taking in first air, continuing to inhale, gestating nine months to inhale. Fingers threads his needle with catgut suture and the newborn sits to her sternum and issues a feint bawl. He stitches the mother back together, the newborn flapping her ears, stars singing hallelujah. Alphonse mends back the uterus employing the special inverting continuous they taught in school. He returns the mended womb to the abdomen, situating the organ in its proper place in the belly of life. Doc stitches the layers of muscle, and brings the skin together, a smooth surgery. He opens the heifer's swollen teats, bringing milk forth, and unties the heifer. She rises. Once risen, a cow lives. The calf attempts to suckle. The dream goes slow motion, the calf bawling, her mama lowing. Fingers gets the calf on the suck, to have the new mama nudge him with her poll...awakening him.

The man in the moon winks, and Fingers wakes up on the back side of another dream to gather his instruments and move on to another cow in trouble. He humps his yellow Impala across open country to the next ranch, giving life like some god of the night. Fingers re-awakens, or dreams he has reawakened. Moondrives rekindle another chapter of his life. His subconscious reels out scenes, his guardian angel speaks, telling him everything is alright, a movie illuminated by the dancing moon, by the stars and planets and all the comets and auroras that measure time...

SUN

Sheriff Oberly loves his wife. He knows Vallerone is older than old now, and slow to return home. Time is all that is necessary, Oberly thinks as he—mnugh—spasms sperm into his grateful wife, shuddering. He lies spooned and considers his loving spouse. She shudders more than he. He imagines his spermatozoon, the lucky one, finding her ripened egg, penetrating, fertilizing, two cells becoming a zygote, a new life. O feels the beat of his wife's heart, her womb contracting, an ovary shedding the ovum, spermatozoa on their journey. They nap in their orgasmic coma, their act of procreation. Oberly re-dreams a childhood dream. His wife giggles and pushes him out.

'My father could die out there,' Oberly recollects Ricky saying, 'my father could die!' The statement reverberates in his skull; Oberly sensitive to the things people say, dismissing nothing. Ricky had listed the ways; 'hypoglycemia, hypothermia, heart attack, stroke, car wreck, flood, a trampling, a kick to the head.'

If Vallerone's end was going to be by a kick to the head, he'd be dead long ago. The man knew hooves. To avoid hooves, he had learned to think like a horse and cow, and did. Oh, the beatings animals give a healing man, the chaffing. Vallerone's life winnowed on, his world thinning, senses failing, the animals knowing him, the old doctor knowing them. There had been some recent Vallerone trouble, the sheriff had to concede. A few months back Oberly had pulled Fingers over for a traffic violation at a stop sign. Actually, Fingers was stopped at the sign, asleep. A Good Samaritan had reported the doctor unresponsive at the wheel, twitching. The caller called to request the sheriff help his friend, reporting the veterinarian's car running, Fingers asleep at the wheel, foot resting on the brake. 'Gone,' the caller said Vallerone looked 'gone.'

Within minutes of fielding the report, Oberly wheeled in, pulling his Crown Vic bumper to bumper with his friend's older model to keep the car from rolling off. He thought the vet's heart might have stopped thumping. Sheriff Oberly didn't want a runaway car driven by a corpse romping though Conrad, as it wouldn't be the first. He reached in through the window and slipped the gear shift on the console into park. He nudged Fingers, massaging his shoulder to wake him. Vallerone came to, slowly. He looked good, not pale or gray, but pink and oxygenated. Oberly surveyed the gathering of souls, relieved his pal hadn't departed the world altogether.

"He's okay," Oberly announced. "On your way. Move on, please." The folks didn't respond to his request, not just yet. Oberly hadn't expected them to leave the sideshow. Conrad was a quiet town. People didn't often sleep in their cars at stop signs midday.

Fingers gazed ahead, assessing his situation, his location; stop sign, Main Street, hands on the wheel. When he had a bearing on the world, he spoke. "Okay," he said, "I'm fine. I'm headed home." A car passed by, and another, the hum of wheels on pavement mesmerizing him to sleep in the first place, mesmerizing him again...and again he nodded off, even after Oberly's awakening, as if he couldn't help it. Not good. The sheriff rubbed him awake. This wasn't right. He's afflicted.

"You don't seem right, Doc. You've come down with narcolepsy, it seems," Oberly suggested.

Doc V didn't reply. He looked off, nodding in half agreement. Bird watched him mull the possibility, tonguing the notion.

"Could just as well be exhaustion," the sheriff added, kindly. Vallerone may have spent the night performing pasture surgery, as he had time and again through decades past. His knife was still sharp.

Gradually, the surgeon gathered his senses. Oberly visited as if to be discussing some official matter, hoping onlookers didn't put too much into appearances, their cars nose to nose and cockeyed. Oberly felt Fingers' bewilderment. The veterinarian couldn't altogether fathom Oberly leaning through his window. Fingers knew the badge and hat. He and Sheriff O met by night, never by day.

"Life's catching up to you, Doctor V," Oberly remarked. "Street sleeping; that's not a good thing."

Vallerone winced.

"A little nap, yes?" the sheriff queried.

The veterinarian smiled. "Yes, so it seems, so it seems. Must have drifted off. " He clasped his fingers to the steering wheel, verifying his awareness of driving.

"Where you headed?"

"Home." Wheels spin by.

"You've been working nights?"

"You know I have," Fingers replied. "Cut the theatrics," he whispered.

"This sleep is gonna cost you," the sheriff declared.

"Cost me?"

"A clear violation of the law," he intoned, assessing Vallerone's reality.

"What law? No law against sleeping in my car."

"Sleeping while travelling?" Oberly dipped a dark

eyebrow. "Some law forbids that. I'll find a law." The small
crowd listened, lingering, the idle curious—Vallerone their
showman of late, his animal heroics of yore, a Lazarus to
some. If not as savior, then as storyteller, Conrad's original
allegorist. And then there were his mysterious
disappearances and imperviousness; that black bag, Swift
Dam, Indians, horses, cattle, and hay.

"Look at this mess you've created," the sheriff scolded
Vallerone. "I'm grateful no one is hurt."

The sheriff went around to the other side of the car,
sweeping the gapers back onto the sidewalk with a swing
of his hip. "No standing in the street. Please, people, step
back if you could be so kind. Thank you."

"Does he need the ambulance?" someone offered.

"No, thank goodness." the sheriff answered. "He'll be
moving on shortly, just taking a brief respite from a long
day at work. Clear on out if you could. Give us all some
air, would you?"

He opened the passenger door and sat in the passenger
seat while keeping his feet on the road, getting control of
the situation as sheriffs garner control. The car, needing
new shock absorbers, sunk, tilting Fingers, waking him
further. He caught the wheel tight with his left hand, as if
Bird might pull him out of the car. Bird flicked open the
jockey box, thumbed through the papers, smiling. Fingers'
license tags were expired. No insurance papers to be
found.

"Unlicensed vehicle," he muttered.

"Puh..."

"No insurance."

"I'm insured."

"You might be, but you don't have the papers."

"Leave me alone, O. Let me go home."

The sheriff persisted, wanting to make sure Vallerone
was good to drive. "I'd like to, but I noticed your brake
lights don't work, either."

"Was I braking?" Fingers asked.

"You were braking, sleeping while braking. Not a bad combination, I admit. Just worried what might happen if one of those nightmares hit you when you are sleeping while driving. Don't want you coming out on the wrong side of a dream."

Fingers looked down at his feet. His right foot was on the brake. Thank God for sweet dreams. "This dozing off is new," he admitted. "What did you call it?"

"Narcolepsy, it's called. We learnt it in sheriff school. Seems you sleep sporadic."

"Yes, now and then."

"You've been nodding off unexpectedly now and then?"

"Yes, sleeping as to dream. Fantastic in its way."

"You've stopped here to have yourself a dream?"

"I guess... dreaming about you, didn't mean to cause trouble. Wasn't sure where the dream ended." Fingers looked at the gallery of people, ancient clients and creditors, a few strange faces, appearances warped by time.

"A good dream, then?" Oberly asked. He opened a bottle of water and bade Fingers drink.

"I believe so." He'd forgotten the dream. "A lot of good dreams. Not a bad way to get old really, dreaming young." Fingers drank the water.

"Youth—that's what you dream about?" the sheriff asked merrily.

"Hope to, yes; even you must know, a dreamer like you."

"Yes, I suppose I do."

"In dreams, age is nothing. Time is nothing. Time wheels, and drags, but dream time is nonexistent." He gulped, inhaled, and caught his breath. He licked his lips and considered his hand on the wheel.

Oberly sensed the doctor's angst. Naps coming to involve others, something Vallerone hadn't expected. He preferred napping in peace, one reason he drove to Swift to sleep.

"There may be a penalty for your condition."
"For sleeping in the street?"
"Yes."
"The state has a penalty?"
"That's right. They'll lift your license."
"This United State?"
"That's right. The State of Montana."
"Which license? My vet license?"
"Yeah, that too. You need checked out. A horse doctor of your sort wouldn't want to lose his license. Wouldn't want to go to sleep looking at a horse, would you?"

Vallerone smiled.

"Horses take care where they sleep. They have another horse or two watching over them. You should consider that. What you need is a chauffeur again. You can't be sleeping vulnerable."

"Might make things simpler to be unlicensed. I'd have a reason to say no to the next heifer in trouble. Maybe I'd start getting enough sleep at home." Vallerone recalled a portion of the stop sign dream. The memory made him smile. He was young in the dream, young again, very young. "I like my dreams."

"Better than reality, are they?"
"Some. Most, anyway."

"You need a wellness check. Your naps—they're getting dangerous. What happens if you fall asleep when you're rolling down the road?"

"I'll get examined," he agreed, the sad day the doctor becomes the patient. He dropped the car into gear, pitching forward, nudging into the sheriff's cruiser.

"You're getting everything checked," Oberly restated, putting his hand on the dash and shoving himself up and out of the car.

Fingers squinted, smiling. People moved closer.

Oberly began his charade and snapped his pen into the writing mode. "Judge or sawbones, what'll it be?" he asked Fingers for all to hear, flipping open his citation book.

"I like that new judge. He liked my book. Write me up a ticket to his big room." Vallerone laughed his raven laugh, and a woman watcher mumbled *crazy loon* loud enough for him to hear. He laughed and cawed. "Not all loons are crazed." Since his novel had come out, Vallerone could not be counted on to talk straight. And ever since the new vets took over, he joked about with everyone, recompense for all the seriousness he had to strut through the years.

"The fine could be up to five hundred smackers. Sleeping while Driving. Your friend the judge won't be looking kindly at this stunt."

"That's way less than a real doctor will cost. Get scribblin', Barney."

Oberly poised over his citation book, laughing to himself. "You know what?" he said, pocketing his pen, "you're going to the doctor no matter what. Sleeping in the street? Give me a break."

"I'm a doctor. I can take care of my health," Fingers proclaimed, his mind awakened. A good sign, Oberly thought. "Write the ticket. I'll discuss it with the judge. I have my rights. I didn't mean to fall asleep. Some things are beyond one's control."

The gatherers thinned, trolling Conrad to come upon another occurrence to ponder.

"Why don't I just follow you home and we'll have your wife babysit the car keys?"

Val sighed and nodded. He was tired. Maybe something was out of kilter.

"I'll stop by in a few days. We'll arrange that trip to the doctor. I'll make an appointment for you. I know those doctors at the clinic."

"I don't need a family doctor."

"A neurologist visits...

"An internist," Vallerone suggested. "I need someone to see inside."

"I'll figure out who to set you up with, horseman."

Fingers licked his teeth and scratched his chin. "Fine," he said, easing off the brake, creeping ahead, pushing the sheriff's car to get the sheriff on his way. "Thanks for your help."

"Thank me later," Oberly said, stepping away.

"I won't be thanking you when the quack has hold of my nuts." This comment scattered the last of the Conrad streetwalkers, sending them on their nosy ways. The sheriff had defused the situation, as was his knack. Fingers sleeping at the wheel wasn't much of a situation to defuse, and their relationship complicated the situation.

"That's what you're worried about, then?"

"I have control of my health," Vallerone re-stated.

"Old Man controls your health."

"So what's the use?"

"Say I set you up with that woman doctor that drives in from Great Falls each week, some sort of graceful-aging specialist, I believe? She'll know how to handle nuts like yours, big guy, and slip in for a feel of that prostrate."

"Prostate," Fingers corrected. "They don't finger prostates anymore; nope, they wait for clinical signs in that department these days. I read up on it." He'd not considered a woman doctor, even though the last two veterinarians he'd hired were woman. Eighty percent of all new veterinary graduates are women. He had lived a long time, indeed. Female doctors show up to help you these days, nurturers with tiny, delicate fingers, women needed in the mix long ago. Oberly slammed the door to snap Fingers awake, to keep him awake. "Take care of yourself, old timer," he said, "I'll pull out from in front of you and then I'm right behind you." He slapped the hood for added effect. "Carbon monoxide could snuff you out next time you pull this stunt."

Fingers sighed. Indeed, not safe to dream with the car running. "Thanks," he said, a bubble in his throat. Oberly pulled his car out of the way. Oberly inched forward, looking both ways. "Thank Napi I was stopped when I went under," he told himself. He flicked on his blinker and crept onto Main Street. Oberly gave a short honk to keep him moving.

Fingers drove home, Oberly tailing. The veterinarian pulled into his driveway, put the car in park, and shut her down. He snatched the keys and jingled them for the sheriff to see. Oberly saluted, and drove on. Doc's wife pulled open the drape to check on her husband's arrival. Vallerone, legal now, opened the door and called his dog, who piled in beside him. Maple watched her husband pet his dog and close his eyes. He dozed. Man and dog. She let sleeping dogs lie.

Vallerone dreams: *Oh time, you whore, stop having your way with me. Your cadence drums my bones, your rhythm warps my flesh. Stop you, stop. Stop fusing the hinges of my back, stop thickening the joints of my soul...*

Fingers enjoyed car dreams with his dog sleeping in the seat beside him. He awoke from the nightmare of age, and slept to dream of youth. He preferred sleeping with his seat reclined. Impromptu sleep provided impromptu relief. As Fingers aged, everything had found its place; his writing, journeys into the mountains, everything but sleep. With life copacetic, he'd become weary of time; a fear of living he'd not previously endured. All his life he had worked on achieving certain goals; a family, a veterinary practice, a novel; all achieved. Only a Kentucky Derby runner waited. He had the cow herd, a ranch was within reach.

He faced an elusive goal, a watery destiny he could not put his namesake fingers upon. He considered that his mind might be weakening. He probably did have some disease. As with most veterinarians, Fingers had diagnosed and treated his personal ailments all his life. He didn't appreciate the benefits real doctors had to offer, or how they offered those benefits: the appointment, arriving to fill out forms and wait, the carbolic stink, insurance forms and questionnaire paperwork, clocks hidden and hard to see, the cover of last year's National Geographic warped with infectious exudates—all to meet some medico who acts weird because he's a doctor and you're a veterinarian, or worse, a novelist.

Fingers conceded that veterinary medicine wasn't able to treat the narcolepsy affliction he seemed to have succumbed. It was no big deal when the family pet slept all day and night; a sign of aging accepted by all, no treatment necessary except a raw bone a day to keep the veterinarian away. Through the years, he'd often counseled his clients regarding prolonged sleep of their old dogs, not so uncommon a problem. In their end, dogs sleep life away. Feed them the best meat and massage them daily. Fingers figured that maybe he was at his end, or the prelude to the end, sleeping his life away like any old dog.

Sheriff Oberly thought the same thing. He showed up two days later and carted Fingers to the local medical center where he'd arranged an appointment with the woman internist. True to form, Fingers fell asleep on the waiting room couch. A nurse woke him and led him through some doors and hallways. She weighed him with one of those balance scales that checks the height. "One hundred seventy-one pounds; five feet, ten," she murmured, recording her numerical findings.

Time had shrunk Fingers Vallerone. Once, when he was young and his intervertebral discs were soft and spongy, he tipped six feet. All the bending and lifting, all the tumbles and falls had worn him down, the animal life shaving two inches off his stature.

She requested he disrobe "undergarments and all." She threw a smock over his shoulders that opened in the rear. She led him down the phenolic hall. He followed like a willing horse. Sans undershorts, Vallerone felt his testicles swing. Bowlegged from all his years in the saddle, his seeds didn't know what to do with all that space. As she led him along, he drew a deep breath through his nostrils and pondered how he could get his veterinary clinic to smell like a real hospital, as if smell somehow conferred competence. Ventilation: veterinary clinics probably lacked the necessary investment in high-priced filters and air exchange systems. Never the smell of urine or feces in a human hospital, while veterinary clinics reek of animal odors; vomitus and exudates, a wet-dog-like stink, cat urine. Perhaps the indiscretion of animals, eliminating and regurgitating right in the clinic, especially when scared and sick, often not offered the walk they needed before arriving. Dogs and cats have no verbal communication, but with emissions they scream.

The attendant led Vallerone to a chair in a windowless examination room. She sat him down beside another table of slick, snotty magazines. The smell of medicinal solvents and disinfectants continued to inundate Vallerone's senses. He sat and considered his life, his health. It wasn't phenols he smelled, but anesthetics, inhalant anesthetics, the exhalation of anesthetic gas by the recovering surgical patients all through the hallways.

A mirror reflected his condition. Not bad for seventy something. Facial wrinkles running deep, but a proportionate physique. He wasn't fat. No, Vallerone's mind alone burned enough calories to keep him thin and fit. A heart had a challenging workout everyday just to pump the blood to a brain like Vallerone's. He kept his body moving, walking and riding his horses every decent day. Horses kept his age at bay. The constant conversation atop them kept his psyche sharp and active and in harmony with his body.

He fished the stethoscope off the exam tray and auscultated his chest, self-diagnostician he. His heart sounded fine. Lub-dub, lub-lub, lub-dub, lub-ub, lub-dub. Fairly steady, save that up and down arrhythmia that corresponded with his breathing. He listened on. His endocrine system reacted to scrutiny, increasing his heart rate. Maybe just a half beat missed now and then. He was not so sure about his lung sounds. Light rales, perhaps a heaviness. He dropped the bell down to his abdomen and listened to the light bubbling of his intestines. Hernias. He was entering the hernia age. He tried to check himself for a hiatal hernia, fingering his stomach, the rim of his diaphragm.

Footsteps paraded back and forth outside, none stopping to read his file. He tried to palpate his liver under his ribcage, but couldn't get a feel of the hepatic margin under the ribs like he could a cat's.

He hoped the doctor knew her stuff, anxious to have a woman attend to his health. His wife, Maple, wavered at the idea of a woman poking around on her husband. Once attendant to his various needs, Maple hadn't attended to anything regarding his person lately, his evasiveness as responsible as her disinterest. Alphonse closed his eyes. He did the relaxed breathing. He said his Catholic prayers he'd memorized as an altar boy back in another world and life. *Oh, Mother of the Word Incarnate, despise not my petitions, but hear and answer me, Amen.* High-tech machines whirred beyond. A clock ticked unseen. Fingers fell asleep, again, grateful for the armrests.

He awoke to the smell of those anesthetic gasses, vapors escaped from the surgical suites, medicinal fumes exhaled from the surgical patients gurneyed down the hallways. Gas uncaptured slipping from the machines; gas expired in the exhalations of the patients even after they have returned to their rooms. Everyone in the hospital operated in a semi-anesthetized state, the hospital soma. Vallerone had purchased the modern gas anesthesia contrivances for his young veterinarians. Maybe if the young doctors anesthetized enough dogs and cats, his clinic could someday possess the ethereal smell of a real hospital.

Vallerone snoozed, burying himself in dreams of morbid speculation regarding his health; a malignancy discovered, a condition fatal and incurable diagnosed. He jerked awake, lost for a second, unknowing of where he was, or for a split second; who he was. Dr. Vallerone, hospitalized at last. He'd been kicked in the head more than once through the years, his belly stepped upon by cattle, his hips rolled and body bowled over by horses, his head slammed in metal chutes by cattlemen. Must be the anesthetic in the air, he reassured himself.

He examined his state of existence in the mirror again, trying to replace the image with one from an earlier place in time. Life had altered him. Age brought him to this place, his face turning into a rag, a wrinkled, crevassed rag, a map of one's time on earth. Vallerone pondered how the doctor might arrive at a diagnosis regarding his narcolepsy, if that is even what he had. With what information garnered, in what manner would she determine his ailment? Blood tests, x-rays, palpation, EKG, ultrasound, what? An ophthalmic exam, a look at his tonsils, an anamnesis? Would she auscultate his heart, work off the nurse's history, feel his abdomen, and know?

Vallerone had relied on his fingers all his life to diagnose what burdened animals. He had no radiographic capabilities in the field, no ultrasound, no blood scans, no digital imagery; nothing other than his namesake digits abetted by his eyes and nose, a feel doctor all around, a veterinarian, as they say, telling by observing, by feeling, by seeing through time.

Fingers Vallerone waited at the benevolence of fingers other than his own. A tinge of excitement came with thoughts of a woman doctor palpating him, if indeed she would go so far. He had heard from skeptics that doctors look across the room at the patient and order up diagnostic procedures to determine his afflictions. They send the patient to be scanned elsewhere and wait for a report from a radiologist to read the images, consider the numbers, diagnose the condition, and prescribe what their profession has dictated they prescribe, evidence based medicine. That's how it went when he ran Maple through the medical jungle when she started fainting a few years back. What a ringer. They never brought her around. Most believe it was the medical marijuana that restored Maple's health. Fingers embraced her folk medicine cure.

Vallerone sat and smiled. He had learned that smiling made him feel better, even forced smiles. Finding himself as a patient was a new feeling, a cruel tease. He stopped seeing his dentist because of the relentless x-rays the techs exposed him to in the dental office. This was his first visit to a doctor of any sort in a decade. Medicine had changed since Dr. Hamilton sewed up the tendon he'd accidentally severed doing field surgery on a bull. The bull kicked the scalpel out of his right hand. The flying blade sliced the index flexor tendon of his left. He'd been a patient before. A surgical team in the hospital anesthetized him. The surgeon cut. He claimed to have sewn the tendon back together, but it never functioned normally again. Despite surgery, the tendon lost its leverage on the distal phalanx. Forevermore, Vallerone lost the ability to flex his left index finger at the distal joint, his first taste of the physical demise that comes with time and age. Not a great thing for a surgeon, a flexless index finger. Live with what you have, they advised. The surgeon carried on, maimed by his own surgical doing. His digits adapted. Fingers sliced and sewed, slicing and sewing the flesh of mankind's domesticates, Fingers the surgeon.

He considered the constraints of human medicine. Vallerone enjoyed the free rein of veterinary practice. Animals can't talk, you see, nor lie. Through his years, he enjoyed one the finest medical runs in the annals of veterinary medicine. One innovation after another enhanced his ability and popularity. Cures became commonplace. Veterinary medicine in the 60s and 70s thrived on new techniques and medications, one innovation after the other knocking off diseases that had plagued producers for eras. Vets were awarded DEA licenses, and with drugs became miracle workers. New antibiotics and anesthetics made veterinary medicine safe and effective in deft hands. Vallerone led the wave of animal medical success. He integrated progressive medical and surgical strategies into his practice. He learned what not to do. He revived life where death waited, time and again. He was not the last to let go of the old, nor the first to embrace the new. He did what worked, what cured.

In the end, drugs became overprescribed. The pharmaceutical miracles waned. The drugs-for-all ideology pushed Vallerone away. Where care and feeding had once sustained animal health, medication became the scrim supplanting proper management. Ranchers developed a dependency on drugs and vaccines. Drugs made people lazy; that's what Vallerone despised most. Hormones intensified production. Baby calves tabled, injected with hormones and multivalent vaccines, their hides sizzled with a hot iron. Hormone injections and hot-iron branding of baby calves haunted Vallerone. This was the twenty-first century, and still the branding. With all the progressive medical and agricultural innovations, Vallerone couldn't understand why no one had developed a sensitive and efficient means of identifying animals other than forcibly branding the babies with molten metal. Brutal, barbaric, and glorified, a sorry dominion over the domesticates. And society wonders why rape and violence are community problems. Any child forced to witness the despicable act of calf-branding could not be expected to be reliably non-violent.

Vallerone loathed the lack of compassion. The cattle medication trend drifted into Montana from Iowa and Illinois. Vaccination became relentless, chemical feed supplements routine. Hormone implants. Insecticides. Genetically modified corn. Antibiotics injected, antibiotics in the feed. Chemical dewormers and potent pesticides poured upon the cattle. Needling, and more needling, injections of all sorts, beef production riding a pharmaceutical dependence, sound husbandry submerged in pharmaceutical scrims. In time, beef-borne disease started sickening the beefeaters.

Pleas came for natural production. Vallerone knew natural. He teamed with the ranchers on Birch Creek and Heart Butte. He left the pharmaceutical practice behind to tend Indian cattle, the drug-free approach. Natural wasn't so much his doing as the Indians'. Animal drugs were an alien idea. It was not in the Indian mindset to be injecting Napi's creatures with chemicals. Vallerone recruited cattle buyers for his clients' unsullied calves, speculators offering a premium for the calves raised on organic milk, grass, and water; beef of the purest sort. Heart Butte ranchers had access to wholesome grass and strong water to raise the hardiest calves in North America.

Vallerone helped the Indians produce strong calves. Indians implemented their natural production, while Fingers provided the mineral supplements and forage balancers to round out their grazing health; phosphorus, calcium, trace minerals, and salt. Cattle and horses evolved to graze the grasslands, and the minerals helped them along. With Fingers assistance, the Heart Butte ranchers successfully avoided the drugs and vaccines the irrigated ranchers came to depend upon for production. Irrigation had diluted the health down-country.

Vallerone came to spend days on end with the panhandle Indians. What used to be afternoon trips to ride herd became weeklong stays. As Vallerone moved his cows from range to range, mingling with the Indian herds. Few in Conrad—not the new veterinarians, not his family—asked or cared about his extended absences Swift Dam way, no one at all. Glad to be rid of him they were, he felt, both at home and at his practice.

Vallerone sat, contemplating his future as a patient, the rise and the fall of his personal health, his flagging vigor, the narcolepsy affliction. He heard delicate footfalls stop outside his door, a silence. He took a deep breath and awaited his examination. He heard hands shuffle his scant medical record, not much to see. Vallerone was not on any medication, nor was he allergic to any drugs. No tests had been run in years, no radiographs, nothing, a clean slate. No diseases, no medical misfortune of note that his veterinary toolbox hadn't mended or cured. No surgery but the finger surgery, no infectious disease other than the lingering but mild Brucellosis he picked up from the Strain 19 vaccine. Vallerone had been a lucky man. Health accompanied him on his rounds, vigor his ally. When he had become sick, he'd treated himself, dosing himself at the first symptom, no time for illness as a country veterinarian, not until now.

A crescendo of anticipation rose inside his chest. His heart galloped, changing leads. The time had come, the door opened. A pleasant internist stepped into the room holding his chart high in the air with one hand, shaking Val's hand with the other, signaling him to stay put with a gesture of his chart, like one might signal a dog to remain sitting. "Hi, Doctor Vallerone, I am Dr. Sally Jo Schroeder."

Fingers, taken by her presence, could barely respond. "Pleased to meet you," he managed. He stared, adoring the woman under the stylish smock and medical skirt. He wondered what made her include Jo in her professional name. Sally Schroeder sounded professional enough, Sally Jo, he didn't know.

She set his medical record on the counter, placing her hands on her hips to size him up. "What brings you here, doctor veterinarian?"

"I was coerced," he replied. Fingers looked at her hand for a wedding ring. Seeing none, he attempted to stand. Taking command of her new patient, the doctor steadied Fingers, placing her hand on his shoulder. She grasped his elbow with the other hand and eased him back in his chair. "Relax, let's just take our time here. No need for you to stand, yet. Just loosen up a bit, will you, please?"

Vallerone took a deep breath and resigned himself to her ministrations. He took the weight off his feet and sat back on the chair. She stepped to his side, her fingers never leaving his shoulder. She massaged his neck, assessing flexibility, much like Vallerone might unwind a tense horse. As he relaxed, she palmed his hand, checking his pulse in the small of his wrist. Fingers took another breath and closed his eyes. Nice bedside manner, real nice.

The doctor went about her examination, peering into his ears and nose with her otoscope, and quickly. She gazed into his eyes with her ophthalmoscope. She set the instrument aside to palpate his head and neck, feeling about his jaws and under his throat. She handled him deftly, making some notes in the record after feeling a swelling in his gullet. She had him rise and walk across the room to the exam table, assessing his gait. She sat him up to have him lie on his back, easing him down like a wife might put an ailing husband to bed, but not like Maple put him to bed. No, he and Maple had separate beds, and of late, separate bedrooms. Vallerone had moved to the guest room some time back, all his going and coming at night taking its toll on her sleep, the phone-ring conditioning losing its charm. Maple moved the phone into his room: no more ringing in the night for Maple. The woman doctor palpated Fingers' abdomen, kneading his abdominal muscles checking his diaphragm, palpating deeper organs, the type of physical exam Vallerone appreciated. "Nothing like a good feel of the giblets," she bantered.

"How has your sex life been?" she asked, as if to read his mind. She slipped down to feel his gonads, avoiding his penis. Vallerone didn't know what to say, as this was something he had not planned on being asked, as if it were out of the realm of medical, which of course it is not. She talked with precise movements of her tongue, fingering his testicles as if they were an instrument and she a musician.

"Sporadic," he replied, considering Birch Creek. She rolled him on his side, assessing his ribs and spine. He felt himself fade, feeling he might fall asleep. He wanted asleep. In the doctor's hands, he wanted to go to sleep. In staying awake, he realized something might be wrong with his health, laid out before the doctor; naked and old and sleepy to the touch. 'There will plenty of time to sleep in your grave,' he remembered Many White Horses telling him when he recently nodded off up North. That sleep might not be far away, he considered, not far away; he in the hospital, part of the medical industrial complex now, in hands other than his own.

The doctor rolled Vallerone from his side to his tummy, applying a special pressure to make the transition painless. He could not stop comparing veterinary medicine with human medicine. Veterinarians envy human doctors, all their conveniences, their high salaries. Vallerone did not envy real doctors, not this one trying to figure him out, his heart thumping, his mind open.

With all the doctor's note-taking, Vallerone realized a veterinarian had the freedom to diagnose and treat like no other medical professional, practice unhindered by accountability. It had been a pleasure to know by looking, to treat without pause, to skip the notes and records, no time for that. Veterinary medicine meant efficient medicine in Vallerone's hands.

Vallerone could hear the rolling of her pen, the dotting of i's and crossing of t's. The she-doctor percussed his ribcage with piano fingers. She auscultated while gently tapping, she the raven, his torso the window. Vallerone welcomed the stroking of his intercostal muscles. Sally Jo knew her way around a body—after all she was an osteopath, a DO. Perhaps he had been too pessimistic about human medicine. She demonstrated concern and feeling. She rolled him to his back. She checked his psoas muscles, pressing deep into either flank. She nudged his bladder from either side, and swept the rim of his pubic bone with a finger so light.

Fingers identified the logo on the stethoscope that

hung from her neck; a Littman stethoscope similar the one he used to hear inside animals. She checked his inguinal lymph nodes and his inguinal canal for hernias, walking her fingers up his ribs to his armpit, across his chest, and back down the other side. She smiled and murmured as if to imply 'such a healthy old man,' so Vallerone mused.

She felt his jaw joints and temples again, as if their disposition might have changed during her exam, and perhaps had. Vallerone felt changed. The exam was changing him, something about the doctor's touch. She pressured his jugular groove with an index finger while auscultating his heart, assessing how the heart beat matched up to the carotid pulse. She spotted the head of her stethoscope on various parts of his chest, listening carefully at each stop, she switched from the membrane side of the stethoscope to the bell, and listened some more.

She stood him over and took some deep breaths herself, as if the examination was a laborious effort. A labor of love, Vallerone felt. She smiled down at her patient before stepping behind him, stroking the underside of his neck. She thumbed his clavicles and slowly felt down his sternum and the rims of his ribcage. She tucked her fingers under his costal arch to skim the edges of his liver, and then down to his flanks to thumb his kidneys and finger the nuances of his aging digestive tract. Fingers came fully awake, examined for the first time in his life.

Dr. Touch washed her hands and re-gloved. She sat Fingers up and torniquetted his arm and rolled out a set-up to draw blood. He felt thrilled to have the doctor draw his blood. As the exam proceeded, Vallerone considered human medicine perhaps not so different from veterinary medicine, at least with Sally Jo at the helm. Her needle fell into his vein; the sensation sexual, a whimsical penetration of his doctorness by hers. Blood issued into a succession of glass tubes she slipped in and out of her blood-collecting sleeve. "Nice looking blood," she said, holding a tube to the window.

Her needling of his flesh filled his mouth with wetness. As she withdrew the needle, a nervy jolt ran up his arm, as if she'd brushed a nerve with the surgical steel. She taped gauze into the small of his arm, and flexed his elbow. Fingers tingled. Footsteps approached outside. A quiet knock. Dr. Schroeder answered, "Come in," her voice hypnotic. The physician looked Fingers in the eye, her bedside manner assessing not only the physical, but also the mental, the behavioral as he would call it. With animals, Vallerone evaluated the behavioral first, and then the physical. Animal behavior was incredibly telling for Vallerone. He learned the animal talk well. Animals told him where they ailed, helped him see. Never lied.

The assistant entered the room and labeled the blood tubes. The needling seemed to awaken Fingers to some heretofore hidden inner life. The doctor's prodding and pinging informed him of his aging existence, but the needling enlightened him. She kept up the note-taking, as if writing a book, The Life and Times of Vallerone's Bones. "Seems your thyroid gland is bit enlarged, nothing really out of the ordinary, worked over by time some. Sometimes iodine intake runs low in these inland parts. Sometimes you get too much, perhaps from handling drugs containing iodines or iodides. Goiter, you know."

His neck had felt a bit full of late, an odd tightness to the delicate wattles that had begun to form under his jaw. He wanted to hug her when all was said and done, but in the end simply thanked her, "A pleasurable examination, Sally Jo."

Her diagnosis came back as hypothyroidism. Fingers' thyroid gland had petered-out, confused by his day-versus-night existence. The thyroid dysfunction had caused his metabolism to slow, not all that unusual in older men. A life lived by night, the recent novel drama; time itself had wrung out Vallerone's metabolism, or so Sally Jo proffered. Fingers' medical mind figured the impaired thyroid function was possibly the result of the thousands of x-rays he'd taken of horses and dogs and cats. It's not like he could tell Fifi or Seabiscuit to hold real still for the next ten seconds while he left the room to trip the x-rays from a safe distance. He absorbed more Roentgens in his day than recommended. To him, radiation was the best explanation as to why his thyroid function had faltered. He had goitered himself; taken too many radiographs of fetlocks. He handled a lot of iodine as well. Intravenous sodium iodide was one of his favorite horse and cow remedies, strong stuff, and curative. Perhaps his iodine exposures had something to do with the thyroid sleepiness.

His other organs tested out worthy; a happy heart, succulent kidneys, and a pert liver. She'd checked over his entire skin surface, most all of it. The only other trouble issue was a slightly elevated blood glucose and a hemoglobin test that suggested the glucose had been high, off and on of late. The way Vallerone's cerebral cortex metabolized energy, it was no surprise his glucose fluctuated. Vulnerable to diabetes, perhaps, but not yet diabetic.

In the end, Dr. Sally Schroeder prescribed thyroid hormone, levothyroxine to be exact, 0.1 mcg/twice a day. Maple had the prescription filled. Doc's friend, the goatherd who ran the health food store, suggested he start on some sea kelp to give his thyroid gland a bath in natural iodine, iodine from the sea, the sea. Vallerone didn't figure himself to be short on iodine, so he passed on the kelp. He did begin drinking goat milk, however, savoring the richness.

In the weeks to come, Fingers responded to her therapy. His speed of living lifted out of the doldrums. He was off and running like a fifty-something again, wide awake by day, sleeping at nights, eating a fresh, natural diet to manage his blood sugar, and walking, lots of walking with his dogs. Riding his horses into the mountains, always riding, riding still. Oatmeal, he came to crave oatmeal for breakfast before his rides, brown sugar melted atop hot oats. Bacon made him sluggish and eggs dragged him down. Fruit: fruit was what his body needed to age gracefully. He became a fruit eater, fresh fruit, which these days seemed fresher and fresher, even in a backwater town like Conrad. The health food store in Choteau carried organic cantaloupe, strawberries, salads, and all the fresh fruits and veggies. Seafood delivered twice a week from Great Falls, Doc became a salmon-eater. Maple was reluctant to switch out all her meat and potato routines to cook up the new diets, but she quickly came around when she figured it out how the health food made his sticker peck out.

The fountain-of-youth action inspired Vallerone, which amused his wife. He bounced around a youngster. Meds can be a wonderful thing. The townsfolk took note of their rejuvenated novelist. He marched around town with his dogs, headed through the fringe cottonwoods exploring all up and down Pondera Creek, the sluggish, fishless stream skirting town. He rode his horses and moved his herd of cattle around more than they needed moved. After a few months of hormonal rejuvenation, the honeymoon response faded, which Dr. Schroeder indicated was not unusual.

"Try to find a balance with your pills and activity and diet," she told him over the phone.

Concerning mortality, Vallerone's visit to Dr. Schroeder had aroused his concern for graceful aging. He didn't want to burden his children. He wanted to stay strong until the end, and then pass off quick and smooth. Vallerone needed something better to worry about than his health.

"Get moving," she urged. "Keep moving. Metabolism is all about moving. Easy on the carbohydrates. Go paleo, meat and berries. And greens."

Vallerone pledged to do what it took to stay healthy.

He ate right, always had, really. Did she need to see him again?

"No, I don't need to see you again," Dr. Sally Jo replied. "Next year. Stop by the lab in a few months for a blood test to check the thyroid levels. If you feel sick, or things aren't right, I want to see you, but if things are going well, just keep going, keep moving. Live with what you have."

The moondriving to Swift Dam became part of Vallerone's keep-moving campaign. Driving, riding, moving cows, sitting with the Indians, meditating his way through time. Pondering, pondering the past, Vallerone remembers Swift Dam, the horses, women, and children.

SHINE

*M*aple Vallerone smelled tension. She could see heat waves rise off the hood. The officer of the law had been running the roads about the countryside. Cold blooded, she felt the police-car heat waft across her porch, heat she'd felt before.

Sheriff O stepped out of his official car and gently clicked the door shut, so as not to alarm Maple. He walked to portray calm, so he might ask a question or two. She stopped swinging and smiled, admiring the streamlined rack of gumballs on this car, none of them flashing, for which she was grateful.

Maple hadn't thought to worry too much about her missing husband. Death crossed her mind as the lawman marched down her sidewalk, accidental death. Alphonse had gacked and the sheriff had arrived to inform her of his unfortunate passing. She had often speculated about such a day. Sheriffs parked their cars in driveways to inform people of dead relatives, yes they did.

She composed herself, knowing better than to take up with morbid speculation. She acknowledged the sheriff with a nod and resumed rocking, shading her face from the sun with a cupped hand. The sheriff climbed her steps. She welcomed Oberly, no great surprise to see him. He had been here plenty of times before, always to see Fingers, never her, never the boys. She hummed quietly, rocking. O began with quiet questions. When did Fingers leave? Where to? Why? Maple listened without replying, relieved Fingers hadn't been found dead. Oberly knew to let her have a moment. He waited as sheriffs wait for people to gather their wits. When she appeared ready, he asked again: "Did he tell you he was leaving for the night? Where he was headed? Why?"

"He might have. I don't remember."

"Any reason anyone should be concerned?"

"You know as well as I this is nothing new," Maple replied.

"Any recent family troubles between you or the boys?" Oberly asked.

"You think we did him in, eh?" She laughed.

"No, no, but Ricky seems upset. Is there some reason you're not forthcoming with more infor—?"

"The flood; he's obsessed about that Flood of '64. You should know as well as anyone what's been going on inside his head the last fifty years."

Oberly didn't know.

"He read about last night's forecast for big rain in yesterday's *Tribune*. Took off to see for himself," Maple explained. "If the dam goes, seems he wants to go with it, the old coot."

"Yes, a lot of rain they've been having up in the mountains there. And atop the snowmelt. Same as 1964, they say."

"It smells so nice after a rain," Maple interrupted, inhaling the morning aroma. "Don't you think so, sheriff?"

"Yes." He breathed and smiled. "He left alone, then, did he?"

"Yes," Maple answered. "As far as we know, he left alone. Always leaves alone. He's not always alone out there in the night where he goes, though, you know. Not always alone I don't believe." This was the first Oberly had heard her use a tone like that.

Maple scooted to the corner of her swinging sofa, tilting it askew, her eyes distant. She gazed at the mountains, a nice view of the Front Range from her porch, much like Oberly's picture-window view. The sheriff and Maple said nothing. They studied the mountains assessing how much rain had fallen on the snow, how much snowmelt runnelled off under the rain. Rocky Mountain Front people have a tendency to stare at the mountains, mesmerized on a regular basis by their grandeur. "He left late yesterday afternoon," Maple said, "after the weatherman forecast heavy rains," she continued. "Orographic rain."

The two of them continued to look outward, as if they might spot Fingers driving home, Oberly standing, Maple on the edge of her swing. A breeze in the trees, the after-rain air sweet as Maple proclaimed. "'Not this much snow and rain since before the Flood of '64,' he declared before leaving," she said, talking to the mountains as much as to the sheriff. "Always comes down to that lost week in '64. Didn't come home after several days. I thought he ended up drowned himself, dead, me waiting for a sheriff like you to deliver the news."

She stares with her mouth open. "That searching still seems to be going on, Sheriff. He's not getting away from Conrad. It's more than that. He's searching for something up there in those mountains, something lost." She murmured some other sentences, ideations Oberly could not string together.

"Searching. Searching still?"

"Something remains unfound."

"Something unfound?"

"Something yet to be found, rather."

"I wasn't born until after the flood," Oberly related.

"Right," she said. "That's right." She looked at Oberly,

gauging that he didn't know firsthand about the flood, not like she knew, not like her husband Alphonse knew. "One night missing is nothing. He was gone seven days and nights back then. Kept quiet a long time afterwards. Then the typing started. Seemed to free him up to live in the present, all those years of typing, hoping someday to craft a story, *the* story, his story. What makes a man want to tell a story? Why can't one be happy reading stories instead of writing them? What a price one pays to write a story. Wife and kids pay."

"But a fine story, Maple, Fingers wrote a fine story. We need stories. Think of it as something good come of the flood."

Maple inhaled.

"You admire his storytelling, don't you, Maple?"

"I suppose I do. He knits the yarn. I helped edit all those sentences, you know."

"A story well told."

"Well told, all right. We hashed over the words for decades."

"People like the novel."

"Some people do."

"I like the novel."

"Sure you do," she said.

"Are you glad they published it?"

Maple gaped at the Front. "The advance was nice. We never considered any trouble with the check in hand. We embraced a mood of smooth-sailing ahead."

"But you're still happy they published it, right, after all that's happened."

"What's *all* happened?" she asked. "You hinting the sailing hasn't been all that smooth, Sheriff?"

"Well, you know, this happening, him leaving, gone half the night. Ricky riled. People talking..."

Maple stared at the mountains. "People have always talked." Maple had heard talk.

"Yes, and still they talk. Talk is how it can be for a

writer," Oberly put in.

"Publish something and it's out there to read and talk about, that's sure enough right, sure enough."

"Some say what they please."

"True enough."

"Too true around here."

"What goes around comes around."

The novel hadn't brought Maple much. She had had all she wanted before the dang book; a home, grown sons on their way to prominence, tincture of marijuana. Maple held her gaze west, projecting her mind into the cordillera that bewitched her man, pursing her unlipsticked lips, sliding them back and forth across her teeth as if something inevitable was happening up there, again. Swift Dam, somehow responsible for everything that had gone wrong the last fifty-some years of her marriage. Swift Dam.

"He didn't stay out all night because you and he had a spat or something, did he?" Oberly asked, half-heartedly.

She gave him a look. "Didn't you already cover marital discord?"

"Oh, come on Maple. These are just the questions I'm trained to ask. Don't take it personal. It's part of the investigation your son instigated when he called in the middle of the night to report your husband missing. Seems he is going to follow up on how I handle his missing person report. I am here handling the missing-persons report."

Maple puffed.

"Well?"

"You know as well as I that I'd never kick him out," she said, as if she was privy to all the conversations he'd had with her husband over the years. She kept her gaze away, her forehead creased, an eye squinted, lips moving. "We're old now. We don't fight anymore. There is nothing left to fight about. He doesn't fight. He stays out of everyone's way and takes his medicine. He does his part."

"What about the bag?"

"Bag?"

"His black bag—the doctor bag."

"He brings the bag with him everywhere. Used to need a sedan full of tools and potions, but now he just needs the black bag."

"And yesterday?"

"With him."

"And inside it?"

"Heaven only knows."

Oberly clicked his tongue off the roof of his mouth and took a deep breath. He didn't relate well to wise women. Even his relationship with his mother Tess remained ambiguous at times—the lost father. Elders in his Heart Butte clan were seldom asked hard questions by the young, no probing questions at any rate, only respectful questions designed to seek knowledge and guidance. Oberly was dealing with the woman who knew Vallerone best of all. If she didn't know what was in the black bag, it was because she didn't want to know.

Maple eyed the sheriff's pistol. She surveyed the dents on the holstered Billy club. She winced at the thought of police violence, of gunfire, clubbing, and Tazering. With a flick of her hand, she dismissed the sheriff. Oberly understood, he thought he did. Actually, he didn't understand her sudden alienation. He backed down the steps and sidled to his car, keeping his eye on her as trained.

He considered the midnight phone calls the veterinarian's wife endured through the years, all those heifers in trouble, all that sexual resonance. Before getting into his car, Bird smiled and gestured politely. He looked sharp in his ironed slacks and official jacket. She nodded in return, a wrinkling of a lip, her incurvated grin. Most humans had lost track of the gesture language embraced by animals, where the slightest gesture tells the biggest truth, but not Maple. She knew Oberly knew a lot about her husband, and she also knew that he didn't know everything. Neither fully understood the basis of the other's smile, only that their smiles regarded Fingers and all his complexity, what he might be up to this time, how it will likely end up all being okay, or so they both hoped. Their smiles reflected their relationship with Vallerone—what each knew of the other—and of Vallerone, their knowledge of his secret life as a moondriver.

Oberly sat deep in the seat of the cruiser. He sensed Fingers had let Maple in on plenty about himself. Seemed he had. The sheriff started his car and saluted goodbye, enough fieldwork for the time being. They'd give Fingers some time. Maple stepped down to the driveway. She gestured Oberly to stop as he backed away. She had something to add, something to ask, or tell. Maple was a wiry woman, fit from all the daily walks up and down the outlier roads each day with her pack of pariah dogs. Her early-to-bed, early-to-rise lifestyle had drawn her into the winter years nicely. Dogs kept her fit as the horses kept Vallerone fit. She leaned into his window from behind, mimicking the sheriff's method of speaking to halted drivers. "He's still trying to put the pieces together from the Flood of '64," she intoned. "You are one of the pieces, it seems."

Oberly kept his eyes straight ahead. He'd heard the rumors. "Like I said, I wasn't born 'til late that winter following." His hands sweated on the steering wheel.

"Maybe you could do me a favor," she asked.

"What's that?"

"As part of your investigation this time—as long as it's come to that—find out what sort of Indians he hangs out with up there. Which Indians, or which Indian?"

"Now that sort of information is readily available in his book, isn't it Maple?"

"His book is fiction."

"He hangs out with the flood Indians."

"The Native Church people?"

"That's not what I said."

"But isn't it the Native American Church he visits?"

"I don't really know, Maple. Peyote happens. He hangs out with the ranchers, the horsemen he works with. His horses graze up there. It's out of my jurisdiction, you know."

"Ha!"

"Religion is a funny thing up there. Church and nature get mixed up some. I myself generally stay out of the church side of things."

"Your mother lives up there."

"That's right, my mother and Uncle Howler, too. They still have a little slice of land on Birch Creek. Flood of '64 welded them together on the land up there, brother and sister. Someday I hope to ranch their little spread, someday soon, if you want to know the truth. Might not be long before you won't have to mess with me again, Maple. I'll be back with the Indians, where I originated."

"Maybe after you return you'll figure out why you left." Maple stepped away from the car.

Oberly understood Maple despised reservation Indians, a prejudice instilled in her as a child. Her husband loved the reservation, he loved the Indians. He found his place in the world amongst the Indian horsemen and storytellers. Oberly understood the couple's differing views, Fingers having the reservation world to himself, Maple holding down the whitewashed home in Conrad.

Oberly thought over the Flood of '64. What could it mean to Maple? Some loose end untied. The two-way radio squawked, calling for an assist at the jail with an unruly prisoner. He paid his respects to Maple with yet another small salute, and popped his rig into reverse and began his slow roll out of the driveway, gravel popping out from under the slow turn of tires.

Conrad was a quiet town, sometimes too quiet. Maple rubbed her forehead, gazing at the Pondera County watery emblem of justice on the sheriff's car, unclear as anyone about her husband's world out west. Through the years, she accustomed herself to his night absences, most of them veterinary calls. One night was nothing. And he hadn't even yet been gone a full day. She wished the fuss would subside. Hoped her husband would just return. He always had, always had.

In years past, not all that long ago, Vallerone would remain unaccounted for two and three nights in a row without much worry or thought given to his whereabouts. No one filed any missing-person reports when he was out making money, no sheriff sidling in to inquire about family trouble, or to go as far as to insinuate malfeasance on her part. Ha! She'd wait it out like she always had. Not that waiting was easy. Waiting for a husband to return is never easy. She went back into the house and brewed herself another pot of green tea, special tea that helped keep her young, tinctured tea that had delivered her through days past and would deliver her through days present, a fatty tea to soothe the loneliness of living, of growing old.

She remembered well the Flood of '64, her life submerged in the fifty-year upshot of all that loosened water. Such a long hard rain like no other, inches of rain fallen upon yards of accrued snow. After the dam broke Billy James, the rancher/damkeeper, called requesting Fingers bring his horses and come find Howler. Maple fielded the call as she had fielded so many of Fingers' calls. "*He's on his way.*" Always on his way. So began her husband's long missing-person voyage into Swift country that continues to this day. Fingers missing horseback half a century past riding his string down a ravaged river. His horse trip revealed all he ever wanted to know about Manifest Destiny: a broken dam and dead Indians.

Maple Vallerone waited out the Flood of '64 in her kitchen sitting beside her radio, her husband fifty miles away searching for survivors atop his string of sturdy horses. He'd always sought to help with his horses, listing his volunteer horseman status with Search and Rescue. The young Dr. Vallerone and his horses disappeared into the foothill wilderness of the Rocky Mountain Front, the reservation hinterland. Gone for days, a week, and Maple Valerone waits still.

"A man horseback with two pack horses rides the riverbottom," the airborne reporter announced. She remembered how the KSEN announcer kept pronouncing the 'S' in the word debris in his aerial report. "There is all sort of debri*s* floating down the river, cows and houses and debris." A strange thing to remember about the Flood, the announcer hissing debris at Maple as he reported her husband riding the riverbottom.

During that rainy, snowy week preceding the Flood of '64, Fingers had twice driven to Birch Creek below Swift Dam to help Ivan Buffalo Heart's heifers, the man for whom he searched. Fingers first met Ivan riding horseback behind Swift Reservoir years before the flood when Ivan helped cart Billy James out of the wilderness with a broken leg.

Fingers delivered a calf by cesarean the week before, and when Ivan's second heifer got into trouble, Fingers arrived as he'd always arrived, ready to deliver. More snow than ever waited in the mountains that dulcet spring afternoon, the mountains a sublime white from a winter of snow, relentless snow fallen into the spring, heavy snow.

The heifer waited for Vallerone. The fetal tail hung out the helpless heifer's vulva. Two tails. The backwards baby waggled the tail, beckoning the men help. A backwardscalf—breeched—unable to breach the world tail first. The mother bewildered, knowing to push, but not getting the pelvic pressure required to stimulate her pushing because the calf could not enter her pelvis, a breech malpresentation. To deliver the calf, Fingers would push the fetal pelvis back into the uterus and then bring each leg into the pelvic canal, one hoof at a time. Vallerone would *mutate* the *in utero* fetus, veterinary obstetrician he.

To numb the heifer's netherland, he dropped a needle between the vertebrae into the epidural space at the base of her tail. The negative pressure inhaled the anesthetic. With his left fingers, he pushed the calf's rump. With a right arm, he reached beyond into the uterus, cupping a distant hind hoof into his palm. He flexed the hind leg, *folding*, retrieving the distal limb and pulling the hind hoof into the pelvic canal and out the vulva, a miracle maneuver, the cow doctor's art. Likewise, he fished and *folded* the other hind leg, flexing and mutating the limb into the pelvic canal, theriogenology at its finest. He rotated the calf inside the uterus to allow a quick exit once they began pulling, this to avoid aspiration of placental fluids into the yet-to-breathe lungs. Vallerone wanted the calf out alive. He placed straps on both hind legs to extract the fetus, to bring life into the world, again, once again. With the heifer standing, Ivan Buffalo Heart and Doc Vallerone rotated the calf out of the heifer's womb.

In unison, as if practiced, Ivan Buffalo Heart and Fingers lifted the newborn high in the air to drain fluids the calf may have aspirated during the rearward delivery. They laid the calf on some clean snow. Fingers left the calf hooked to the mother, allowing the placental blood to enter the calf, waiting minutes before clamping the umbilical cord with Carmalt forceps, stimulating the calf to inhale deeply. Fingers cleared the mouth and nose of mucous. He pressed the chest gently to assist breathing. He blew softly into the nostrils of the baby. The calf snorted and sneezed and bellered and began living on her own, our god of the night delivering, soon on to deliver another, and another.

Vallerone stayed to visit with Ivan Buffalo Heart, to commune with the new man of a domesticated land. From the river cabin window, they watched a delightful swirling snow blanket the foothill ranch, a fresh layer of white, the mountains radiant as ever, a new storm chroming the peaks each week. Snow, snow, snow. As the veterinarian and Indian rancher warmed, Ivan told the tale of water, her spirit to be free. When the story ended and the snow didn't stop, Fingers decided to head home. Ivan Buffalo Heart invited him to spend the night on Birch Creek that night before the flood, to hear another story or two, but Vallerone had other heifers waiting in other valleys. By the time Fingers made it home, several feet of white jeweled the Front.

Clouds spun up from the Gulf of Mexico. Wet weather moved in. After their cumulus journey across the heartland of America, the charged and saturated Atlantic clouds bumped into the Rocky Mountains. The mountains pushed the clouds to new heights, *orographic lift*, the meteorologists said. The gain from three to eight thousand feet in a span of twenty foothill miles brought on heavy rain. A long hard precipitation, heavy rain, relentless rain atop all that snow high in the mountains. To add calamity, an Arctic front fell down from Canada with more precipitation. More rain on top of more snow. Compression and meltdown—the curse of Napikwan. Unalterable water.

The tyranny of mankind gave way to the fluxing watershed. All-consuming water subsumed the dam, breaching the blockade as Ivan's story foretold. Old Man predicted water would prevail over all, as water once had. An eighty-foot water wall rolled over the riverbottom, ravaged the Indian ranches, drowning all downstream. Fathers and mothers and children, storytellers drowned. Water remains undefeated.

Fingers loaded the horses he'd bred, raised, and trained and trailered west. He left his pleasant home in Conrad, departing to save the survivors. It would be his horses' most important calling in life, and his—more important than the ranch calls and pack trips that preceded the flood, more important than the roundups and cattle drives that followed. He rode to rescue the Indians, to find and save the survivors; his mission. Vallerone, seven nights missing back then.

Fifty years ago—fifty years to the day—Fingers parks

his car under Swift Dam. The hard rain of '14, a controlled and managed flood with a sturdier dam, a concrete parabola. Fifty miles away, Maple rocks on her porch, '64 as '14. Then as now, a yearn in her eyes.

Fingers sits in his car mourning the drowned Indian, Ivan Buffalo Heart, the rancher he'd brought two calves forth the week before the Flood of '64, live calves. He remembers Ivan Buffalo Heart's voice, Ivan dead too many days to speak, too much mud and water and heat for the man to have talked, all but his soul disfigured.

Fingers remembers the stories Ivan told before the Flood of '64, the same story he told after the Flood of '64, the same story over and over. Ivan told the story years before the flood when he packed broken-legged Billy James out of the wilderness. He told the story again after the breech delivery. Fingers feels the words, Ivan's Indian lips resonant.

Time has a hold on Fingers, time and age, the snow is melting, the rain falling. The new dam gets stronger with each additional inch of precipitate. With each new hour of runoff the concrete becomes mightier. 'The more water she's asked to hold, the stronger she gets,' the engineers proclaimed, just like the engineers for the old Swift Dam proclaimed; she'll hold water forever.

Water swallows everything,
Water swallows all.

Water has her way
With the whole world.

Like a frightened horse,
Frightened water breaks free.

Water pours into the reservoir from the Rockies. Snowmelt, rainwater. The Gulf of Mexico moisture making its roll all across America, the Arctic moisture dipping down. Elevation incites rain to fall, and fall she does.

The spillway spills a waterfall over the far shoulder of Swift. The original dam had water spilling over its top, hydrodynamics that quickly destabilized and dissembled the earth-fill. Vallerone stares upward. He watches the new dam through the drizzle, his bones pained by the rain, joints in need of ambulation. He walks, walks to lubricate his joints, to stiffen his bones, to condition his muscles. He knows locomotion is the key to longevity. To keep living, one must keep moving. All of the animals taught him that to move is to live. All becomes dependent on locomotion in the end. When you stop moving, you stop living. When the water stops flowing, all is over.

The rain fades and the sky clears. The moon has hiked into the sky behind him and shines from the east, brightening the trail into the wilderness, illuminating a path he will seldom travel again. His children no longer want to ride with him. There are no grandchildren, but he has dreamt one is on the way. He knows to be grateful for memories, and is. He thinks of Tess and her brother Howler Ground Owl, the ones who lived. He remembers the drowned.

Vallerone moves. He wants to keep living, to live long and healthy. He does not want to let life go, not yet, nor youth. He puts youth into his steps as he climbs the trail that rises to the reservoir. He breathes, his heart dances, happy to fuel his systems with oxygen. He steps out, hiking upward, steady he goes. He does not stop to rest until he stands atop the shoulder of the ancient cleft. The dam holds the water, tremulous. His heart thumps, a buffalo heart.

Ivan's wish for buffalo to return has transpired. Vallerone helped the Indians acquire the herd. Ivan Buffalo Heart never saw a buffalo graze, not in his lifetime. Buffalo graze yonder. Buffalo, cattle, and horses. Deer, elk, even the grizzly bears graze. The spillway spills phosphorescent whitewater into the moonshine, water diverted, exchanged for fiber and protein, for carbohydrates, for bread and potatoes and pasta. For beer.

Parabolic and moonlit, Fingers weeps if weeping is what men do while reconstructing their past atop a steeple of concrete. The dam weeps. The world weeps. There are no tears, only mist, mist everywhere. The concrete shouts into the moonlit night. Moon clouds flit by, throwing shadows about. Fingers breathes. He lies down and is pulled to sleep again in accordance with his fluctuant metabolism. The systems responsible for the hike up have requested a rest. Alphonse does as his body tells him. He lies down and closes his eyes and meditates. The practiced meditation drifts to sleep, and dreams, and... Alphonse Vallerone is again young, not yet named Fingers, but Alphonse! He rides young horses, he teaches the horses, knowing how to teach horses. The horses teach him. Learning and teaching, where did all that animal living go? No one wants to learn anymore, no one wants to teach. The Indians teach. They taught Vallerone, and he hopes to learn more, to teach others.

He tries to wake up and walk about, but cannot arouse his muscles out of their sleep. The night is heavy, the moon bright. Not quite sleeping, he swoons. He rolls over and smells the stone mixing with water. He curses the monolith, raising a defiant fist. The parabolic concrete does not care. It gathers moonlight, deflecting it upon Vallerone. The sky above is blank, the stars dissolved by refracted light.

The rain has stopped. He manages to open his eyes. Across the cleft, spillway water splashes over the shoulder of the canyon wall, the overflow stirring a froth at the base of the dam. The spillway waterfall mist roils up, touching him, becoming him. Vaporized water stirs a pool at the base of the dam before gushing beyond, rushing down the gutted riverbed, a riverbed not yet recovered from the eighty-foot wall-of-water gashing it took in '64. Fingers dissolves into the Flood. The moon reaches its apogee, holding court over the mountains that feed the reservoir. Night is sucked into the swirl of water at the base of the dam. The atmosphere of time and memory hypnotizes Fingers. He finds himself flat on his back. He dozes—a missing person sleeping. He dreams visions he can and cannot remember.

Midnight passes quickly. The moon beats down from straight above, stars dissolved by Moon. Water tumbles and whorls, the old man narcolept. His dam of Old Man dreams has broken, burst. Life spills down his shoulders. His head rests on a rounded rock, his thinning hair a scant pillow. His legs splay, fingers spread on bedrock. His liver rests loose inside him, the moonglow loose without. He breathes deeply, and dreams.

Listen: Is he talking in his sleep, or is it a soft snoring? Perhaps he is weeping again. The old man spindles his own electricity, neurons circling and gyrating within. A whimsical expression adorns his face, wrinkles of time piled upon folds of memory, runnels of good stretching through the rough.

Look: His eyeballs jitter and jerk under their lids. He dreams deeply.

There: A corner of his mouth quivers, wetness accumulates. He sucks and sits up to reposition his body to dream another chapter of his life. He licks his teeth and opens his eyes. He rolls over and rises to his hands and knees. He looks down at the dam and understands where he is, but not when. The spillway shouts at him from across the cleft, drowning the night in angry water. Twenty inches of rain in the two days before this trip to Swift Dam, precipitation after a wet blizzard the week before, wet spring snow, same snow that covered the mountains in '64, snow atop which Gulf rain came falling, water melting and then swallowing everything, uncapturable water. Nothing got stronger fifty years ago but the water. The water story reels through Fingers' mind, vivid and real.

Beware. Old Man's Water
Cannot be harnessed.

Not like your horse or dog.
Water is a woman.

She cannot be stopped,
Cannot be tamed.

Napi knows Water,
Knows She cannot be tamed.

Old Man knows men try,
But cannot tame Water.

Ivan Buffalo Heart told the story the day before the Flood of '64. But it was not the first time he had told the story to Fingers. Fingers remembers that the first time Ivan Buffalo Heart told the story was when Ivan Buffalo Heart helped transport the damkeeper Billy James out of the no-man's wilderness behind Swift Dam. Decades ago when Ivan Buffalo Heart and his cousin Many White Horses encountered Fingers trying to pack out the broken-legged Billy. The Indians met the Alphonse as he came over the Continental Divide from Big River Meadows. The two Indians helped the teenager transport Billy out. Billy James fractured his femur in a horse mish-mash and could not walk. He could not ride. The trip off the Continental Divide became tortuous. When Indians walk out of the wilderness transporting a broken-legged, drunken white man, stories are bound to flow. Blue moons ago, blue moons gone... Alphonse remembers.

See here: The aging Vallerone opens his eyes; he cannot discern memories from dreams. He cannot tell story from reality. Which side of the dream? Perhaps it is his age, the age that Indian stories become reality. Maybe it his medical condition, a pharmaceutical predicament, an untoward sequelae, a high blood sugar. Perhaps the roar of the spillway has overwhelmed his senses taking him through time past, although never did that spillway spill like this one. So long ago it was when Billy James called, the same broken-legged Billy Ivan carried out of the wilderness singing the water song to Vallerone. He sang the story of the land, time within earth.

Fingers' dreams have no chronology. Time is jumbled. His life is pushed to another dimension, no more or less than reality itself, a vision of memory stacked atop time. On the morning of June 8th of 1964, Billy James, after sending his family to high ground, hiked this same switchback trail up the canyon's south wall to monitor the flood, the same trail Ivan Buffalo Heart and Many White Horses carried him down years before. The Old Man story of water and mud and man aches in the hollow of Billy's mended femur. He hikes up the trail in the rain and sits above the faltering dam. He sees Ivan's story, the water. He rubs his broken bone. Ivan said the dam would break—all dams someday break. But this was Billy's dam, and he didn't want it to break. He knew people downstream that lived on the river. He hoped the warnings arrived in time. They did not arrive in time. He rubs his bone as Ivan's water swallows all.

Billy stayed with Swift as she broke. He witnessed the failure, counting it his failure. The rain came, the snow melted, the reservoir filled like it had never filled before. It was impossible to know where all the Indian families had made summer camp. Sun Dance time approached, more rain than ever before, Gulf rain, Arctic rain, water washing the world, swallowing earth and wanting more, taking it all back—water spilling over the top of the concrete scrim of *his* dam, taking the dam, undermining it.

Billy sat regarding water, the story clairvoyant, Ivan's words. Through the ache of his broken leg he wept, he as helpless as the dam in attempting to capture nature.

Raincoat, cowboy hat dripping, no whiskey this time, none; Damkeeper James' leg aching, his dam gone, washed away, taken by the rising estuary of the great inland limestone sea above. Billy had his spillways ratcheted open, not enough spillway to handle the meltdown. He watched the water fill the spillway, then spill over the earth-filled dam, the water affliction. The whorl bore down and dug out the landfill under the concrete lip, a vortex swallowing the earthfill like only water can.

Billy prays and stays above the dam. He waits, nothing to do but wait. Not often a praying man, Billy James the damkeeper prays that his dam won't give way... he has sent his wife to warn the others. He prays for the Indians he knows the water will smother. As the dam gives—he watches it give—he knows people will die, and they do die.

Something dies in Billy James. His leg aches, evermore the rain will make it ache. Ivan's story trapped inside his femur. After the dam breaks the ache never gives way. As far as his femur is concerned, the rain never stops falling, water always rising. The story inside his leg bone forevermore.

Fingers and Billy rode regular behind Swift Dam, taking their horses into the mountains, young men packing in, escaping Manifest Destiny, trying to, their horses showing them the way as horses have shown men the way through time, the men letting the horses show the way. They rode around Swift Reservoir's tidy water and coursed into the wild world beyond, exploring uninhabited mountains. Billy's faithful mountain mare leading them, his packhorses carrying their abundant gear. Their horses allowed backcountry comfort if not elegance—a big tent and comfortable chairs, warm sleeping bags and fine food. They lingered for weeks in the wilderness in the dray pleasure and secure company of horses, a wild they needed. Bears and elk and nobody but horses and dogs behind Swift Dam during Vallerone's vet school summers.

The two mountain men had the 'Bob' to themselves into the 60s. Few ventured beyond Swift Dam before it broke, save Vallerone and Billy and the vision-questing Blackfeet. Years rolled by, water diverted, farmers happy, backcountry horsemen content, Indians lost. The fifties disappeared, a swift decade. They worked their jobs, Billy ranching and damkeeping, Alphonse schooling, the Indians ranching and riding their ponies all over the range.

One fall they snuck into the mountains in September, up the North Fork of Birch Creek, on by Kill 'em Horse Canyon. Their faithful string of horses carried them up the Continental Divide and over Badger Pass (mountain sheep grazing in the dusk, unafraid of horses or men that high in the void), and down the switchback (a wolverine scrambling into the twilight). To Strawberry Creek, spawning waters of the great Dolly Varden, the September-spawning Bull Trout. They arrived at the Arbuckle Camp by dark, darkness nothing to the horses that led them in. They bivouacked under the Milky Way, Billy building the fire wandering men have built for eons to provide heat and safety, to keep the wilderness at bay. Alphonse brushed the horses down, putting them to grass.

A great ditch of wilderness. Billy and Alphonse, horses and dogs—a big empty full of wildlife. The old man re-dreams it all, reweaves that particular trip into this night. No one talks in this dream, this is not a talking dream, or hasn't been so far...

But watch Fingers' lips, listen: A mumbling works out of Fingers' sleep, Billy James howls from Strawberry Creek. The painful words enter Fingers' dream, loudly. A stomp from Billy's lead mare snaps Billy James' femur. She spooked as she drank out of the creek. Startled from behind, she bowled over Billy, stepping on his femur and breaking his leg in her flight, a scramble to escape the bull moose that had sauntered in to drink downstream. A long way out of the mountains to haul Billy James and his fractured femur. The smoothest way out was the longest way; down Strawberry Creek, through Gateway Gorge to Big River Meadows. From there, over the swale Continental Divide and down the South Fork out to Swift Dam, a smoother summit than the switchbacks up and over Badger Pass to the North Fork.

The schooled Alphonse tried to splint Billy's leg, but the fracture was too high. Billy needed a full-body cast to stabilize the problem, a toboggan. Fingers considered leaving Billy, riding out and bringing back help. Billy said no. He wanted out of the wilderness, didn't want to be left alone in the uninhabited expanse. He claimed to be willing to weather the ride out.

Fingers thought travois. He devised. He chopped, stripped, and tied two sleek lodgepoles to the saddle horn, and dragged them around behind his gray packhorse, acclimating her to the idea of travois poles dragging behind. Fingers didn't want any more troubled horses. After he habituated the gray to dragging the poles, he made a body-length sling by stringing a sleeping bag between the struts. He dragged Billy aboard. At Gateway Gorge the trail narrowed and wouldn't accommodate the travois. The Great Plains horse-sled was too wide for the tree going. Not much to do but drape Billy over his horse, belly down, and walk the gray out.

Billy's ride draped over the gray horse jarred the shivered ends of his broken bone, motion grating shards of bone, traumatizing his nerves. Muscle ripped with each step; shifting, scraping bone. Billy James felt the agony, whiskey his only anesthetic, and plenty of that. Delirium, a quart and a half of whiskey to kill the bone pain of Billy James. Through Big River Meadows the going came smooth. Alphonse stopped to rest and graze the horses. He laid Billy out on the soft grass, and re-rigged the travois.

Fingers met the questing Indians at the Continental Divide, Billy James comatose. The Indians stepped aside, and waited for the horses to pass. The Indians often rode their horses, but not this vision quest. The travois dragged empty, Billy draped over the gray. Ivan Buffalo Heart and Many White Horses watching the empty travois drag by. The Indians trekked to quest for vision, but ended up packing Billy James down the divide, saving his leg, if not his life, Firewater Billy deranged by pain and whiskey, rescued by Ivan Buffalo Heart and Many White Horses.

Many White Horses knew Billy James as the damkeeper, the orchestrator of diverted water, sacred water. He'd gentled horses for him. Ivan Buffalo Heart had met Billy on the river below Swift Dam. Billy fed Many White Horses on an earlier vision quest, succoring his starvation with a grouse stew on Cox Creek up Beaver Lake way. Many White Horses had no vision. Near starved in a cold rain, he owed Billy a favor for nurturing him out of the wilderness.

The two Indians removed the travois poles dragging behind Fingers' gray, converting the travois into a hand-held stretcher. They rolled Billy James onto the stretcher. The pedestrian transport softened Billy's grind. Down the mountain the Indians marched. As the trip wore on, Ivan Buffalo Heart sang the water stories; *water always getting her way, water swallowing up the world.* Water.

The singing Indians delivered the crippled mountain man to his dam, a damkeeper saved by the Indians. Billy had long gone silent in the stretcher, the pain softened by stability and whiskey, the Indians knowing the trail, hiking him down the mountain, understanding whiskey well enough, glad he'd drunk it all, happy the suffering man slept.

Fingers rode ahead of the smooth-footed Indians listening to their water stories. He thought Billy might be dead, so quiet and still he had become on the march out. He was afraid to stop and check, or to interrupt the stories Ivan sang.

The footfall of horses echoes in Fingers' ears, hoof beats of memory. The Indians shuffle behind him. Ivan's stories spill down the mountain like water.

Beware of Old Man's Water.
Water cannot be harnessed.

Not like your horse or dog.
Water is a woman.

Certain flows
Cannot be tamed.

Old Man knows water.
He knows She cannot be tamed.

Old Man knows men try.
But cannot tame Water.

Swift Dam fails. Napi's water escapes. Indians washed afar, washed away.

Time and nature heal the geologic scars. Nature rebuilds the wilderness a season at a time. Men rebuilt the dam. Birch Creek seeks natural. Signs of the great flood disappear over the years. There was no Noah; no Ark. Trail crews streamline the wilderness. By the 70s it became a different wilderness, more people. White people. No one mentioned the Flood. As if it hadn't happened. But it did happen, could happen again. An earthquake could shake the dam loose, another snow-blown winter followed by this big rain.

WHAT HORSES KNOW

*H*ere we wait: Fingers is young. He remains Alphonse. He is summoned to the Flood of '64. He rides the ravaged riverbed searching for survivors. He came to find the living, his horses and dogs sniff for the dead. He rides hard, the sun shines harder. A Swift wall of water rolled over the world; the riverbed a mudded, graveled void; a wasteland. Ridges razed, tree groves torn asunder. Homesteads floated away. Herds drowned. Pigs, chickens, cattle, grouse, deer, bear, humans; all creatures extinguished. Lives lost forever.

Sky blue and sun hot. Clouds thinning. All the rain wrenched from the sky until no more rain could fall. Airplanes hum high. Helicopters chop their whang, dopplering back and forth. Ravens fly forth, cawing, feasting, and showing Alphonse the reaper's way. Coyotes flank his journey.

Alphonse Vallerone rides with the hope of rescue, to rescue the red man's soul. His horses carry him downstream, across the wasteland. They carry him upstream. Each bend finds more carnage. The search for corpses. The strange hope Alphonse might use his medical skills to resurrect an Indian as he'd resurrected so many of their animals. He carries saddlebags of potions and fluids.

The dead wait to be found and delivered to their kin. The living search. Savior no longer, Fingers rides on. He does not long for his home in Conrad. He does not miss his veterinary practice. He does not worry about his wife. He rides his horses, his family of animals. His dog escorts them along. The horses take him to dead horses drowned by the flood. Vallerone jots down a description of each horse he finds. He draws a portrait of each horse in his notebook. He re-imagines the horse standing, with special note of color and markings. He records the brands on each horse. Some horses lie upon their brands. Others are unbranded.

He reconnoiters with the Indians from ridge to ridge, sharing the description of the deceased horses, ripping out the pages he has painted for them. Indians bow their heads upon seeing Alphonse's sketches, horses a part of their family. Somehow, their dogs escaped the flood, dog-paddling dogs having swum to safety. Dogs waited with the Indians on the ridges, welcoming Alphonse with barks of joy in the time of drowning. Dogs playing sentinel. Indian children and dogs ran to greet him. River folk wait for their dead to return, to resurface. Kin wait to make the dead ready for the final trip to the Sand Hills, to bury their dead, to send them off to Heaven and go on with whatever life remains.

At one stop, a disconsolate Indian explains to Vallerone that the Indian afterlife is not a heaven. The Sand Hills are where dead reside, not happy or unhappy, but waiting, dead and waiting for others to die and come and wait with them. Sand Hills, an inglorious place unlike the heaven of others, just a place, a fact of life; death. Best get the living done in the first life. There is no horse stealing in the Sand Hills, no counting coup, no movement. Some prefer to believe in reincarnation rather than waiting about in the Sand Hills, a more promising afterlife as a bird or bear, or perhaps a Whiteman.

Watch: Fingers sweats out his vision, wrapped in his dream, lost in time. The horse journey into the valley of death is real. Perspiration runs upon his forehead. He recollects the ride for the dead. A tear parts his eyelids, dripping down his cheek. Horses become his spirit. He sees as a horse sees, dreams as the horse dreams.

Startled by the tickle of sweat, Fingers opens an eye to receive a dream within a dream, the salty flow a deceptive measure to simulate waking from a dream. But there is no waking under this moon, atop this dam, only more of the riverbed horseback ride. Mourning Blackfeet sit atop every ridge in every direction on their horses and in their cars. Their dogs wait with them. Alphonse canvasses the riverbottom. His horses walk through wailing children and keening grandparents, past mourning nieces and nephews and cousins and mothers and fathers.

A helicopter pumps in to drop a netted bundle of emergency provisions—canned fruit and beans. Sacks fall from the sky. His horse Jake is skeptical of the bundles. Alphonse relaxes his horse. He loads the sacks of food and coats atop his horses and delivers them to those in wait. The people thank him and he rides onward. He could quit, but a spirit carries him. His horses carry him. The sorrel clops down the riverbed, walking the way. The bay and gray follow.

The horses sniff the air. The horses know. Through the valley of death they carry Vallerone. His dog, Lick, weaves back and forth before them, searching, smelling, exploring. The day has been long and the horses have travelled far and it is time to rest. The flood stones have bruised his horses' fetlocks and soles. Their hocks ache. He stops and brushes the horses. He feeds them whole oats the bay has carried. He leads them to green grass to graze at the edge of the devastation.

Fingers' horses are willing partners. They graze, restoring their spirits. Their fetlocks are tough. He rubs their backs and shoulders and he rubs their legs. They graze all night. They graze nearly non-stop. They stop from time to time. While others are on the watch, they sleep standing, if only for a few minutes. Vallerone sleeps out his vision... waiting for morning, the promise of morning.

The sun is hot early, not a cloud in the sky. Rested, the horses show Vallerone the way as they know to show searchers the way. Vallerone bred and conditioned his horses to have strong bones, to have kind dispositions. He had planned for trips as this into the backcountry, the same conditioning required to win a horse race. He'd never imagined using his horses to rescue survivors, not in his lifetime, not with Manifest Destiny so tidy as before Swift broke.

Fingers had taught the horses to show him the way as men have taught horses through time to show men the way—willingly. A wet heat weighs the morning air. The stray water finding refuge in earth evaporates into the sky. The horses blow and snort. The smell of death penetrates Fingers' aura.

Free enterprise churns up another dream of mankind, another tragic memory. Ivan Buffalo Heart appears in the mist of Swift. Atop a moonlight rainbow, Ivan sings the flood song, the Story of Creation itself, the story of bringing life out of a great flooded land, a land flooded before, a land where life will once again have to be brought about if this rain keeps up.

Ivan sings the story as he sang the story carrying Billy James out of the wilderness that day years before the Flood of '64.

> *Once the entire world was a deep and a constant flood,*
> *No land at all, anywhere. Water everywhere.*

Old Man became sad and lonely
So, he sent a duck down for mud.

A while later the duck floated up,
Expired from the effort to please Napi, dead.

A beaver swam in and wanted to help Old Man.
Napi smiled to the animal more accustomed to underwater
worlds than duck.

Beaver took the dive for mud,
But he too floated up, drowned.

Finally, muskrat arrived to try to make the world.
Muskrat took a deep breath. Having the necessary lung,

Muskrat dove to the bottom,
Arising from the deep with a mouthful of mud and two paws-
full of mud.

Old Man smiled and took muskrat's mud out of muskrat's
mouth,
As well as some mud he'd fingered into his paws.

From the dead duck's bill Old Man fingered mud.
From the dead beaver's teeth.

Old Man juggled the mud and the mud multiplied.
Old Man formed the juggled mud into lands, into continents.

He made a third of the world land with muskrat's underworld
mud.
Expansive lands waited for water to grow the grasses to
nurture the soil.

Old Man laughed and blew and heated up the ocean.
He breathed clouds to ferry water onto the land,

He made giant wolves from mud
And sent them running,

Their footprints making lakes over the lands.
All the animals Old Man Napi made from mud.

And then he made man,
He too, from mud.

He made man and woman
And children to live with the animals.

He made plenty of animals
So man could live in peace with the land.

Listen: Fingers' horse steps downriver, from rocks into mudded silt. Suck, suck, suck go the hoof steps. The drowned swell by the next day, stinking the day after in June sun. Smell returns to this dream. Suck and smell. His horse leads him to the mudded corpse, his sorrel horse knowing the travails of man, the horse facing travails with man as horses have through time. The horse knows the man, Ivan Buffalo Heart, for whom Fingers had recently delivered a calf into the world, a new life.

Muddied.

Look: Ivan is muddied, the world is muddy. Humid, hot solstice days in June. Sun Dance time. Mud. The flood inverted groves of birch and cottonwood and willow. Homes ferried twenty miles downstream, lives ferried eternal.

The dog and horses found Ivan,
The horses carried Ivan to his people.

The dog and horses found Ivan,

SWIFT DAM

Ivan sang the song atop the horse,

The dog and horses found Ivan,
The water song. Fingers witness as

The dog and horses found Ivan,
Ivan sang the water song,

The dog and horses found Ivan,
Along the horses walked,

The dog and horses found Ivan,
Singing the song Ivan sang,

The dog and horses found Ivan,
Suck, suck, suck, the horses walk.

The dog and horses found Ivan,
Napi's water cannot be stopped.

The dog and horses found Ivan,
Water beheld swallows everything

The dog and horses found Ivan,
And looks for more to swallow.

The dog and horses found Ivan,
That is the way with held water.

The dog and horses found Ivan,
What kind of people want to

The dog and horses found Ivan,
Hold the water, stop the flow?

The dog and horses found Ivan,

Water has flowed since the world began.

The dog and horses found Ivan,
Who blocks the flow?

The dog and horses found Ivan,
Water cannot be stopped,

The dog and horses found Ivan,
Water rises and gets thirsty.

The dog and horses found Ivan,
Water gets wild when held,

The dog and horses found Ivan,
And wild water swallows all.

Fingers does not reach Conrad that night, or the next. His mission is to carry the Indian home, a dead-speaker, a songster three days dead. When Fingers and his horses arrive with the body, the Indians wail.

The waiting coroner identifies the victim: "Ivan Buffalo Heart."

The coroner, a white man with authority, takes Fingers aside the wailing, out onto the prairie. Relatives follow.

"So you knew Ivan Buffalo Heart?"

"I know him, yes. Ivan, the storyteller. I delivered his calf last week" Fingers replies, nodding to Ivan's kin, they nodding in affirmation that Fingers and Ivan are friends, animal brothers of a sort. "Ivan talked from right atop that horse there, talked as we walked out."

"Stories?" the coroner asks. The kin tighten their lips and nod.

"The water songs. The story foretelling this flood. This flood here and all floods forevermore." Fingers gestures at the devastation, the stripmined riverbed, and the weeping mountains. "The Indians knew this would happen, knew it was coming, perhaps not when, but they knew; yes, they foretold."

Ivan's relatives nod, knowing dead Indians speak plenty, knowing living Indians the Flood foretold.

The coroner does not know what to make of Ivan telling stories. "He didn't tell any stories. Couldn't have. He's three-days dead."

"He has a wife, no?"

"Yes, he has a wife. Howler Ground Owl's sister, Tess. She is waiting for the news of Ivan, the dead news."

"Ivan told me to say goodbye to her, to Tess," Vallerone declares, uncaring what anyone else thinks, knowing he heard Ivan.

"She waits in town. In Dupuyer. At the saloon."

"The saloon?"

"The rescue center, the gathering place."

THE LIVING

Old Man Vallerone awakens at first light, the same time of day he'd awoke with Ivan's widow half a century earlier. He perches over Swift Dam. He grabs a bottle of water from his pack, swirls it in the sunlight to evaluate turbidity, and swallows the nectar. Sunrise illuminates the concrete parabola below him—altered light. The spillway channels excess water over the shoulder of the cleft.

He stretches his legs and peels an orange. He savors the juicy wedges, a devoted fruit eater on his forays north. The fruit nourishes his system, flushes his liver and kidneys. His heart thunders, strong and true. Ceaselessly, water cascades over the spillway, bearing him into the past. This Swift Dam holds water, as the last one did not.

It was on the fifth day of riding the riverbed during the Flood of '64 that Fingers' horse and dog spotted Ivan Buffalo Heart. The dog told the horse, and the horse stopped and sniffed. Between the horse's ears appeared Ivan, crucified halfway up a cottonwood, suspended in a wickerwork of driftwood. Ivan must have climbed the tree to avoid the water, or perhaps the current trapped him against the thick cottonwood as he swam. Fingers dismounted and took his horses to the edge of the carnage.

He hiked back and climbed the tree. It took considerable effort to extract Ivan from the tangle of branches and wood. Ivan's fingers were clamped around the branches like eagle's talons. The floodwater rose above him, silt settling about his ears and neck, in his clothes and on his skin. Fingers brushed away some of the mud lodged on Ivan's neck. He found more silt behind Ivan's ears and in his long hair. He pushed the silt into his shirt pocket.

He unfolded Ivan from the tree, one bone at a time, digits reluctant to leave their grasp. After an hour, Fingers had managed to lower Ivan out of the tree and into the netting. He wrapped him tightly then brought his gray horse over to introduce her to her load. The mare smelled Ivan as if she knew him, and she accepted him. Fingers draped Ivan over the gray mare and rode the bay. The sorrel followed, protecting the trekkers from behind, pinning her ears at the coyotes following along.

Walking his string down the riverbed, Fingers heard a voice, a cry. He stopped the horses to listen. Only a soft breeze. No leaves to rustle. Onward he walked his horses, the horses clipping across gravel and rock and silt. Further, he heard the voice speak again.

He stopped.

The voice stopped.

He walked and the voice returned.

Soon, he realized that Ivan had spoken. Draped across the gray, he spoke.

Fingers knew the voice. He stopped and took Ivan off the horse. He undraped him and pulled him out of the netting, sat him up on the ground, his back to a tree. He stared at the Indian, and then he checked for a pulse. No pulse. Of course there was no pulse. Poor Ivan stank of death.

Fingers carefully re-bundled the corpse. He hoisted Ivan Buffalo Heart back onto the mare. They moved onward. Ivan began to speak again, the gray mare's walk prompting his speech. "Take care of Tess," the corpse implored. "She waits for you."

"Yes," Fingers said.

"The horses will show you her way."

Vallerone felt surreal speaking to a corpse, communing with the dead. Long have Indian stories told of Indians speaking after death...the 'how skeletons became skeletons' stories. Long have living Indians communed with the dead. Vision quests render advice from those passed over to the Sand Hills. Perhaps Vallerone had ridden too long and too hard. Was he having a vision? A flooded riverbed changes a man. Sun and water alter reality. Days spent riding the riverbed, days in the solstice sun, Indians mourning, the lack of proper nutrients, sleepless nights, the wind...

On he rode into the vision quest of collapse.

Ivan spoke again: "You know me."

"Last week, I delivered your breech calf." Fingers said. "Before that, the Caesar."

"Yes you did, my friend," Ivan replied. "You cut the first out, then flipped the calf inside the heifer. Once a horse medicine man, you turned up as the cow medicine man," he laughed.

Vallerone considered: I have found the man who knows me as the cow medicine man. He talks to me in death.

"Thank you for bringing the second calf into the world without the knife," the horseback corpse squawked, clop-clop, clop-clop. "We thought you might cut the calf out as you knifed out the first."

"I only knife out the calves too big to be born. The last calf wasn't too big, she was breech."

"Breech, I know, like Swift Dam... Blocked. Breached. Broken."

The horses walked on, Doc atop the bay, Ivan atop the gray, the sorrel at his tail. Ivan talked; Fingers listened. The four-beat walk, clip-clop, clip-clop; the horse's four beat walk prompting Ivan to talk.

"Tess will guide you. Your horses will take you to her.

They will find her. Horses know how to find her, how to help her. Take care of her, cow medicine man. Take care of her..."

Ivan's voice weakened. Over the miles he stopped speaking altogether. Fingers delivered Ivan to his people. He then rode on to Dupuyer to tell Ivan's wife, to inform Tess.

Fingers recalls the gait by which his horses carried him to her, an animated walk, an amble he'd seldom felt them take. The horses knew. They carried him downstream. They carried him and they carried his gear; the horses carried Ivan's wife's grief, her beauty, her resolve. Falling, the world fallen. He was falling, she fallen. She fell into Dupuyer as had he, felled by the Flood of '64. They plunged into an abyss of loss. Grief welded them together, grief of the terror of water, water sparing them and drawing them into one another.

Fingers holds Ivan's widow. He tells her what Ivan told him to say. He explores the length of her spine with his fingers. He gives her the silt from his pocket, the silt from Ivan's neck—the mud, the mud of life, mud of death, mud of her drowned man.

She rubs the silt between her fingers then puts her fingers into her mouth, tasting the silt, the last of her husband. She holds Fingers Vallerone. He gives her more silt, the silt of the world, spreading life everywhere, silting life from death.

In the early light of a new day, Ivan's widow rests enfolded within Fingers' arms in the pasture beside his grazing horses—two people numbed by the Flood, numb to the world, horses numb from walking through gravel and mud. In time the numbness recedes as the water recedes. Grazing heals the horses, and the horses heal the horse folk, as they must. Ivan and Tess ride onto the rising plains, away from the Flood of '64.

The morning sun is bright, and in brightness the dream

swirls. Ivan's widow wants to hear the story her husband told Fingers, again. Fingers recites Ivan's water story. She wants another story, a sun-child story. Tears fill her eyes and burn her cheeks, dripping hot. He cannot tell the difference between dreams and time, between tears and rain, between moonlight and sunlight, between stories and dreams. He cannot tell the difference between new dams and old ones. He cannot tell what the night brought, or what this day might bring; or what a night fifty years ago wrought.

Conjured memories slip away, and he dreams of Indians with smallpox and tumbling buffalo. He understands that it is not he dreaming his vision these are Ivan's dreams. With Ivan's widow in his arms, Fingers sees the ephemeral struggle: a world gone, a civilization vanquished, a culture washed away.

In the end, a child cries to wake Fingers. A plume of water squirts out the base of the dam. The spillway roars. Water howls. The rain falls, then stops falling. The sky clears. The moon rises and falls. All night he has dreamt. He walks about on top of the dam.

Daylight takes him into 2014, the Year of the Horse. The reservoir is full again. His children are grown. They do not ride with him anymore into the wilderness beyond the trapped water. Billy James is dead. The Catholic is dead. Mother Nature is sick. Howler is old, his horses fewer. Fingers Vallerone hikes down the switchback to his car, gravity pushing him as gravity pushed the water of Swift Dam down the riverbed. Fingers drives out of the cleft and heads east down the gravel road. The past night seems a lifetime. Must be getting old, he thinks, an awful lot of water through the cleft.

The familiar Crown Vic approaches from the east on the gravel road coughing up a great plume of dust. Fingers recognizes the sleek profile of the new gumball apparatus on the sheriff's roof a half-mile away. Their cars converge and come to a simultaneous halt. Bird smiles, happy to find his missing person.

"People are looking for you."

"Which people?" Vallerone asks.

"All sorts of people. I've been looking for you," Bird declares.

"Where're you headed?"

"To my mom's place."

Fingers feels a weight lifted.

"You might be my dad," Bird Oberly declares.

"Your dad?"

"Yes. You: my father."

Vallerone knows to listen.

"Mom and I had a long visit this morning on the phone after I visited Maple, a visit a long time coming. She says you're most likely my sire."

"Sire? When did she tell you that?" Fingers queries, squinting.

"This morning," Oberly says. "After I talked to your wife. She hinted as much. I called Mom to find out if she'd seen you around these parts. I'd figured you'd headed Swift way."

"Your mother told you I was up this way?"

"Yeah, that's right. She told me most everything regarding Swift Dam, past and present. You visit her, always have. Don't know why either of you kept me out of it."

"I guess we just weren't sure."

"You bringing her things all these years?"

Fingers nods. Things. He tilts his head back toward the mother's place, affirming her presence across Birch Creek. He is not surprised she would be telling her son this information on this morning—it was in his dream, Fingers' water dream, a dream not a dream anymore, a dream come to life. Fingers does not speak, cannot speak: wonders what made the mother tell her son that he was his father this day.

"Your son started all this. Called you in missing, you know," Oberly adds.

"When?" Fingers asks, looking to the sun, trying to gauge the time of day.

"Four this morning."

"Which son?"

"That youngest boy of yours."

"The youngest, huh...?" Fingers says, contemplatively. "If what your mom says is true, that'd be you now, wouldn't it?"

"Your other youngest, then," Oberly replies with a grin. "Ricky."

"Ricky never wanted much to do with me after he grew up."

"Sure wanted to know where the blazes you were last night. Seems you've been slipping off with his inheritance or some such shadiness. Is that true?"

Fingers stares at Bird. Something about the way Bird's lips move when he talks reminds Fingers of his own father. The picture of paternal resemblance in Bird is clear, a resemblance pushing through the swarth skin and dark hair.

"Do you believe you're my Dad?" Bird asks, after another spell of silence.

"Yes," Fingers answers. "I held your mother after the Flood of '64. We've kept in touch."

Bird stares at Fingers.

"I promised Ivan Buffalo Heart I'd take care of her," Vallerone explains. "She came to me after the Flood, you know, after he came to me. Well, I came to her. It was a tough time. She rescued me and my horses in Dupuyer as I rescued her. Rescuing became the norm after the Flood. Where one could not be rescued, others were rescued. Ivan Buffalo Heart could not be rescued by me, or by anybody, so your mother rescued me and my horses, and I rescued her in that human way that men and women rescue one another."

"You needed rescuing?"

"Seems I did. My horses did. They'd walked long and hard. Your mom needed rescued. Talking to the dead is perilous," Fingers stated.

"Search and rescue. Your son Ricky wanted me to alert Search and Rescue, but I wouldn't cave to it. Came to see for myself."

"Your mother and I woke up in a pasture the day after I found Ivan Buffalo Heart. I went to visit her the next week, but she suddenly remarried a schoolteacher named Oberly. She needed the safety of a husband. I was another's husband.

"And then a baby came. She gave you Oberly's name. Not long after, husband Oberly departed. He took a job at another school, a bigger, better, whiter school, leaving you and your mother. He was a mathematician, you see. Some said he figured you came too early to be his progeny. Uncle Howler helped raise you, made you the horseman you are."

"So in your novel, that mixing of Indian and White, that was about me?"

"You'd know better than I. You're the Indian."

"Yes, I am. And you're the white father of the halfblood. No coincidence your story patched together our existence."

"It's not like I knew what I was writing, you know. Stories emerge from a place unknown."

"You wrote like a father. The father of an Indian."

He squints at Oberly, the sun glaring. "Maybe I did know. Your mother wouldn't fess up to it, didn't deny it either... No one can blame anyone for anything that happened after Swift gave way. We were all just trying to survive."

Oberly looks to the cleft that harbors Swift Dam. "To think I was spawned from such a flood of water," he declared. "Should we find out for certain? Blood tests will tell."

"That's up to you and your mother."

"Do you need to know if you're my real father?"

"Do I need to know? Not really."

"Is it important to you?" Oberly asks.

"It's important, but I don't need to know," Fingers answers. "I know enough."

"Then you know..."

"I see my father in your lips."

Oberly touches his lips. "I guess I'd like to know for certain," he says, looking away.

"Your mother knows."

"She would know."

"Yes, she would."

Oberly rests his forehead on the steering wheel of the Crown Vic.

"You okay?" Fingers asks Bird.

"I'm okay."

"Well, I better be getting on, then," Fingers says, understanding okay. "You say they're expecting me at home?"

"Yes, they are," Oberly replies. "Your wife and Ricky are waiting."

"As your mother waits for you..."

Fingers eyes Oberly. Oberly eyes Fingers. All along their Pondera County journey they'd felt connected, all those nights, all that travelling, all those animals tended together.

"What's this about a black bag?" Bird asks.

"Which black bag?"

"The black bag you cart in and out of the safety deposit lockers at the bank. The black bag Ricky is so concerned about."

"Oh. That bag."

"What's in it?"

"Funny you should ask," Fingers replies, a grin wrinkling his face. "The promise I made to Ivan to take care of his wife, that's what's in the bag."

"You've been providing for Mom all along, then?"

"As much as I could manage. More lately, with the royalties and all."

"And me?"

"Oh, the place goes to you. She's spent all her years building up the ranch for you, you and Nan. Go see. She's built you a home, a house to call your own. She knows you are better suited to tend grass and cattle than to sheriff white folks. I believe she knows best. We've put a bunch of cows together for you."

Bird smiles. "I thought they were your cows."

"Part mine; mostly Howler and your mother's. I watched you grow up all along, you know. Didn't have much of a hand in your raising, not until you landed in Conrad. Your mother knew what she was doing when she gave you Oberly's name and sent you to school in Dupuyer. She knew you'd end up with some rancher's daughter. She wanted you to have a ranch, and she still does. You won't be going to your wife's family ranch; you'll be bringing her to your family ranch."

Oberly pinches the bridge of his nose.

"When your mom saw that a ranch around Conrad might not happen for you, she decided to try to carve out a lay of land up here for you. In the meantime, she thought time off the reservation might give you some insight into the world. She wished a good life for you in Conrad, but she always hoped you'd come back when there was something to come back to. She's getting close to having enough grass to support a little family like yours."

"So that's why you were so passionate about getting me elected sheriff in Pondera County? You did it for her. She had you stick your neck out to support me in that first election. It cost you several good clients, I know."

"I tipped my hat your way. Not that any one man can get an Indian elected sheriff in Pondera County."

"Seems you did..."

"Your opponent had losing coming to him. You were a

winner. He was a loser. "

"How so?"

"He wasn't nice to horses."

Oberly gazed north. "I suppose it's time I get things sorted out with her once and for all, face to face."

"She just did what she thought was right. She said I was up here, did she?" Vallerone asked, again.

"Yes, she did."

"I'm glad she's talking about the Flood. Fifty years is a long time to hold back water. I had to leave it up to her to tell you. It was never my place, you know."

"I think Nan and I have a little one on the way, that's her sense. She usually senses right. That'd make you a grandpa."

"Congratulations. You've long dreamt a child."

"That bag was full of money, then?"

"Tess and Howler liked cash. They could buy a calf here and cow there with cash in hand. The bag carried deeds and leases, legal papers, bills of laden. Stories, I carried stories in that bag. We had to retain those Indian lawyers in Cut Bank. There are more papers to be delivered, more legal work to be done. We've put some nice grass together for those cows. Tess acquired both leases and deeded land, both sides of the river. You're all set to ranch. I wouldn't worry about the election. Swift Dam, you can worry about Swift Dam."

Oberly drops his cruiser into gear and motors Swift way. Down the road, he turns north, guiding his rig down a prairie road and over the metal bridge across Birch Creek leading to his mother's place, his ranch. Grass grows. Hay waits in the stack. Cows graze, calves play. Corrals solid. Horses. A new home. A new life, a ranch resurrected.

Fingers accelerates east, into a rising sun. He thinks to put Oberly in his will, thinks that might be the best way to affirm the news of the immaculate conception of '64 to Maple. She's waited fifty years without asking for the truth.

Did he even know the truth? Enough truth. Bird's mother had withheld what she needed to withhold. It had taken another hard rain to help her find the will to inform her son. The Flood of 2014 floated up truth, the flood that never happened, a flood of dreams.

Fingers pulls over in Dupuyer and parks. He walks down the abandoned alley to the pasture where he grazed his horses after the Flood of '64, where they found the grieving widow, grief a dance to draw the last of Ivan Buffalo Heart back into her, Fingers bestowing Tess with Ivan's silt, with his own silt.

Silt happens as dams give way.

The pasture dances ungrazed grass, grass as green and tall as '64. The saloon is long closed, Dupuyer a cocoon from which the butterfly has long since flown. Fingers sits on the grass under the birch where the widow and he slept all that water ago. He opens the lunch bucket he brought along and eats heartily before closing his eyes. He daydreams the reality of waking in her arms in the pasture beside his grazing horses—two humans numbed by the Flood, man and woman numb to the world, horses numb from stalking through the gravel and mud, numbed to again feel alive with another.

...varip, varip, varip—grazing horses, stepping and nipping the grass. Tearing it away with their teeth— chewing, ripping, chewing, varip, varip, varip... grazing, forever grazing, mesmerizing the two. He hears Ivan Buffalo Heart tell him to care for her, and cared he has. Fingers thinks of horses long dead; he hears their footfalls delivering him to Tess, the hoofbeats of memory.

Swift Dam, twice built to seal that mountain cleft. Chasm of life, chasm of death. Fingers never bothered to find out where the name Swift came from. Neither did Ivan Buffalo Heart.

Swift Dam, swift life.

ACKNOWLEDGEMENTS

I would like to thank all my friends, relatives, literary mentors, publishers, and readers who have supported and encouraged my storytelling passion through the decades. From my earliest memory, people everywhere have shared their world with me, in particular the Blackfeet, bestowing me with a pulse to share my view of Rocky Mountain Montana in the form of stories.

I am indebted to my parents, as are we all. Rib and Pat, gone now—but never forgotten on any given day—provided me with a childhood of love, beauty, friends, landscape, animals, books, adventure, and wonder, as did my siblings Wylie, Barr, Erik, and Kris, the editors of my life. My children Connor and Nina, along with our dwindling family of pets and horses, supported my writing all along like few muses ever have, or ever will.

This fictional novel was written in honor of the victims of the Flood of '64, the dead and the living.

Grateful thanks to my editors at Open Books, David Ross and Kelly Huddleston, who embraced and refined this story.

All of the events and characters in this novel that emerged from my subconscious, save the Flood of '64, are figments of my imagination. Any resemblances to the living or dead are happenstance.

Silt happens, you know.

Made in the USA
San Bernardino, CA
27 September 2017